UNBORN

RACHEL MCLEAN

Catawampus
press

Catawampus Press

catawampus-press.com

JOIN MY BOOK CLUB

If you want to find out more about Cindee, one of the main characters in this book, you can read her prequel story for free at **rachelmclean.com/cindee**.

You'll also be added to my book club and I'll tell you about promotions and new releases as well as sending you new stories from time to time.

Happy reading!
   Rachel McLean

CHAPTER ONE

Kate Mitchell was tired.

Sure, she'd won her case in the Travis County court, a guy accused of reckless driving. If she was honest with herself, she wasn't sure if he was guilty or not, but she'd done her job, finding a crack in the law and getting him off. But it had been wearing. Listening to evidence from the family of the teenager he'd hit when she'd stepped off the sidewalk, staring at the photographs of her bruised and battered body.

Kate's boss, Tom Abad, had been impressed. Juries didn't like reckless drivers. They didn't like people who plowed down teenagers, leaving them in a coma in the prime of life. But Kate had records from the girl's phone: enough to plant reasonable doubt in the heads of the twelve people she'd faced across the bench.

Kate pulled up outside her compact almost-suburban house and winked off the headlights. She took a moment to watch the movement behind the closed curtains of the kitchen.

Sasha would have finished her homework by now and

would be looking for snacks. And Robert, Kate's charismatic boyfriend of ten months, had told her he'd be waiting with a bottle of her favorite Edna Valley Pinto Noir and a takeout Thai.

She hauled herself out of the car, grabbed her bags from the trunk and clicked the lock on her remote fob. She paused at the threshold to catch her breath then unlocked the front door. Quietly: she'd surprise him.

Once inside, she slipped her shoes under the console table in the hallway and placed her bags on the floor. She could feel her hose rustling as she padded toward the kitchen in her stockinged feet.

She pushed the kitchen door open, gently, placing a smile on her face.

She froze.

Sasha, her fourteen-year-old daughter, was standing with her back to the stove, pushed against it uncomfortably. In front of her, leaning over her, was Robert. He was stroking the girl's cheek with his fingers. Sasha stared back at him, her eyes wide, cheeks pale.

"What the hell are you doing?" Kate let the door slam behind her and strode towards her boyfriend and daughter.

Sasha looked past Robert at her mother. Red blotches sprang to her cheeks and she slumped against the stove. Robert spun round to face Kate.

"Kate, honey!" He stepped towards her, his arms outstretched.

"Don't you *Kate honey* me. What the hell were you doing?" She turned to Sasha. "Did he hurt you, sweetie?"

Sasha blinked a few times then ran past her mother. The door slammed once again and there was the thud of Sasha's feet racing up the stairs. Another slam as she hurled herself into her room.

"It's not what it looks like," said Robert. His voice caught on the *like*.

Kate turned to him. "Go on then. What was it? And what exactly *do* you think it looked like?"

He twisted his lips. She could smell fear on him: high and sharp. "She was upset. Some girls at school took her cell. They've been teasing her for her hair."

"What does that have to do with you pinning her to the stove and grabbing her?"

"I didn't grab her. I was trying to console her."

"She's a fourteen-year-old girl, Robert. She hates being touched. There's no way she would let you stroke her face like that."

He shrugged. "Maybe she opens up to me more than she does you."

Kate felt anger boil in her stomach. "Get out."

His shoulders slumped. "You're angry with me. I get it. I'll come by tomorrow, huh? We can work this out."

"There's nothing to work out."

He put a hand out but she batted it away.

"Come on, Kate. It's just a touch. No harm done."

Her eyes narrowed. "Have you touched her like this before?"

"Of course not."

"And tonight, when you're alone with her, it suddenly becomes alright?"

"No. Yes. I don't know. I was just talking to her."

"She was leaning back over that stove so far I thought she was going to fall onto it. You had her cornered."

He drew himself up. "Come on, Kate. You're exaggerating."

She lifted herself up, wishing she hadn't taken off her

heels. "I want you to leave, Robert. I'll send your things on to you."

He grabbed her wrist. She pulled back but his grip was firm. He'd never hurt her before. He'd never touched Sasha before. "You'll regret this," he said.

"No," she replied. "You will."

He leaned in. "You have no evidence, if that's what you're thinking. Nothing you can take to court. You and your precious lawyer buddies."

"I just want you away from my daughter." She forced herself to breathe. "Give me your key, before you leave."

"Glad to." He plunged his hand into a trouser pocket, letting go of her wrist. She took the opportunity to back away, toward the door. She hoped Sasha wasn't listening.

He yanked a key off his fob and threw it onto the floor. "There," he spat. "All yours, bitch."

She pursed her lips but said nothing. She glared at him, trying not to blink, to look away. He met her gaze as he crossed the floor and brushed past her as he reached the door.

She hurried through the door behind him, anxious to make sure he didn't call Sasha on his way out. He glanced up the stairs as he pulled his jacket off the hook, but said nothing. Kate could feel her heart thumping in her ears. She longed to run up the stairs, to go to her daughter.

Robert opened the door and turned to her.

"It's been good," he said. "Shame to end it like this."

She glanced toward the door by way of instruction. He shrugged and stepped out.

She pushed the door closed behind him and pulled all the bolts. She stared at the door, breathless, sweat beading on her forehead.

Upstairs, music was coming from Sasha's room: Beyoncé.

Kate ran from room to room, checking the locks, pulling the drapes. They were safe.

She took deep breaths as she headed up the stairs. She knocked on her daughter's door but didn't wait to be called in.

Inside, Sasha was lying on her bed, her eyes closed.

"Sasha, honey. I'm so sorry."

Sasha opened her eyes. "Leave me, Mom."

"He's gone. He won't be coming back. I'm so sorry for letting him near you."

"It's fine. Go away." Sasha turned onto her front to face away from her mother. Beyoncé finished her song: something anodyne, nothing like her earlier career, the songs that were now banned. The room went quiet. Kate heard a car drive away outside.

She approached the bed and put a tentative hand on her daughter's back. "You can tell me, you know. Anything. If he touched you like that before, if he hurt you."

"Please. Just go." A sob.

Sasha was a quiet, studious teenager who spent much of her time huddled up here doing homework and chatting to her friends on Discord. Kate respected Sasha's privacy. Her daughter hated being disturbed, but this was different. Kate longed to gather her up and fold her in her arms like she would have done just a few short years ago.

"What was he doing, honey?"

"Nothing. Go."

"You can tell me, you know."

Sasha pushed her hair aside. Her face was red. "So you can prepare a legal case?"

"So I can help you. You can tell me if he hurt you, Sash.

If he touched you anywhere else. I won't take it any further if you don't want me to."

Sasha shook her head. "I want to be on my own."

Kate's chest felt hollow. "OK. I'm not going to force you to talk to me. But anything that's bothering you, you can tell me. It's not your fault. Whatever he told you, you did not ask for him to treat you like that."

"I know."

Kate nodded. She waited for Sasha to say more.

"Please Mom. Just go."

Kate bit her lip. She thought of Sasha's father, six hundred miles away with his new family.

"Go," Sasha repeated.

Kate retreated until her back was against the door. "I love you, sweetie."

"Yeah."

"I'll be right downstairs, if you need me."

"I know." Sasha pulled on headphones and lay on her back, her eyes closed.

Kate stifled a deep sigh and left her daughter's room, hoping Sasha hadn't seen her tears.

CHAPTER TWO

Maya watched the young woman step inside her consulting room and make her way to the hard plastic chair on the other side of the desk. She was slim and blonde, pretty in a girlish kind of way, and she gave the impression of being thirteen or fourteen instead of her true age of sixteen.

The girl sat down, her knees together, her hands placed neatly on them. She held her back straight but her head was bowed, her eyes on the scuffed vinyl flooring. The door clicked shut as she sat down and the endless buzz of noise from the hallway outside miraculously stopped.

Maya let the quiet descend over them for a moment. She was glad of the heavy door to her office, of the quiet it afforded. No privacy though: that was broken by the camera in the corner of the room, where the wall met the ceiling.

"Hey," said Maya. "I'm Doctor Maya Henderson. Call me Maya. I'm going to be looking after you while you're here."

The girl nodded but didn't make eye contact.

"What's your name?" The answer was in the file which

Maya had open on the computer screen between them, but a simple question might break the ice. She glanced at the screen and wrote the date in her notes: August 27, 2026.

The girl sniffed. "Cindee, Ma'am. Cindee Adams." She continued to stare at the backs of her own hands. They were pink, as if recently scrubbed.

"Hi, Cindee. Pleased to meet you." Maya held out her hand. Cindee looked up and frowned. Reluctantly, she put her own hand in Maya's. Her handshake was limp.

Cindee's hand returned to her knee and Maya glanced at the screen.

"Do you know why you're here?"

A shrug. The girl's shoulders were slight, her body too thin for her four months of pregnancy.

"Can I assume that means you do?"

Cindee looked up. Her eyes were large and green, and her nose small. "I know why I'm in this place. I don't know why I'm here with you. Ma'am."

"Please, don't call me Ma'am. I'm Maya."

"Maya. Sorry."

"That's alright." Maya smiled. Cindee met her gaze but her expression was as dull as her complexion.

"OK." Maya closed her laptop, an old model that refused to turn itself on two times out of three. She didn't need it for this. "So tell me why you're here."

"I tried to kill my baby." The girl's voice was thin and shaky. "I got caught."

Maya nodded. "Specifically, you were apprehended outside an illegal abortion clinic in Breckenridge. The clinic's records showed that you were due for an appointment just as the police arrived." She lowered her voice. "At trial, you pled guilty."

Cindee nodded.

"As for why you're here with me. Well, it's my job to look after you and your baby. To make sure your health doesn't suffer because you're in jail."

Cindee narrowed her eyes but said nothing. Maya glanced up at the camera. She had no idea if it was ever turned on, but had to assume it was.

"Is there anything it would help me to know, about the state of your health? Any problems with the pregnancy so far? Any conditions in your family which I need to be aware of?"

Cindee stiffened. Her gaze went back down to her knees. She crossed and uncrossed her ankles, her cheeks red. Suddenly the room felt hot.

"I can help you," Maya continued. "It's my job to make sure your health, and the health of your child, isn't compromised by your being here. Let me make it easier for you."

Cindee shrugged. She lifted a hand as if to place it on her stomach. She stopped it in mid-air and returned it to her lap. Maya gave her a weak smile.

"We have another appointment in two days. I'll need to examine you. Check up on the baby." She wondered how Cindee felt to hear her talking about the baby like this. Cindee had been here a week and as far as Maya was aware, no visitor requests had been received. Did she have a family, or had they abandoned her?

"I'll be gentle," she said. "It won't hurt. Just an ultrasound."

Cindee's eyes went up to Maya's face. "No."

"You don't have any choice, I'm afraid."

Cindee shook her head. "No."

Maya put a hand on the file between them. Where was this girl's mother? She needed support. Were there any inmates who might be able to look after her, or did the nature of her crime mean she would be victimized?

Maya had seen plenty of women like Cindee come through here, but none this young. Her arrest had been the day after her sixteenth birthday. Two days earlier, she wouldn't have been criminally negligent. Just the doctor who'd seen her.

"I'll try and make this easier for you," Maya said. "See if there's anyone you can talk to, if you don't want to talk to me."

Cindee shook her head. Her lips were tight. "No."

"You don't want help?"

"I don't deserve help."

"Everybody deserves help, Cindee."

"Not me. I'm a monster. I sinned."

"You broke the law. It's not the same thing."

Cindee pushed her chair back. Maya looked up at her.

"Don't try to help me," Cindee said. "I'm past saving."

Maya stood up. Cindee was heading for the door.

"We aren't finished. I need to—"

Cindee turned. "What do you need to do?"

Maya shrugged. The purpose of the first consultation was to make contact, to remind patients of why they were here, and to tell them about any further treatment. That had all been done. "Nothing more, I guess."

"Thank you." Cindee pulled the door open. There was movement in the corridor; her next appointment. "Ma'am."

The door closed and Maya stared at it, hating herself.

CHAPTER THREE

KATE SAT ON THE EDGE OF HER BED. DAWN WAS breaking outside, light beginning to filter through the pale blue curtains that complemented her bedlinen.

She stared at the object in her hand, disbelieving. She was thirty-eight years old. She had a teenage daughter. A career. And an ex-boyfriend who she suspected of assaulting her daughter. This shouldn't be happening.

Robert had seemed like the perfect boyfriend. Smart, funny. No ex-wife to worry about. Great job. He'd joined the campaign against AVA, even. He'd seemed to like Sasha and she him. Kate knew he would be no replacement for Julian but hoped that he and her daughter could be friends. She'd loved him, even if she'd been too scared to say it. She'd thought about their future.

On the floor at her feet were three more of them. Four pregnancy tests in total, all different brands. Two had a blue line. One said 'pregnant'. Another had a pink heart.

She put a hand on her stomach. Of course there was nothing there to feel yet; she knew from her pregnancy with Sasha that this thing would be the size of a pinhead right now. No more than a collection of cells, unrecognizable as a potential human being.

She heard the bathroom door slam.

"Sasha!"

She bundled the pregnancy tests under her pillow and hurried into the hallway. She was still wearing her robe, at this time of day.

Sasha was rumbling down the stairs, throwing her backpack over her shoulder.

"Did you have breakfast yet, honey?"

"I'll get it on the way!"

Kate knew better than to believe this.

"Come on, sweetie. There's plenty of time. I'll make you some granola. Blueberry."

Sasha screwed her nose up. "I hate blueberries."

"It's your favorite."

A shrug. "I'm not hungry."

Kate threw open the door to the fridge. She grabbed a smoothie and pressed it into Sasha's hand. "This will keep you going till lunch."

Sasha looked at the bottle like it was a grenade, but shoved it into the top of her bag nonetheless. She sniffed and looked at Kate as if this was the first time she'd noticed her.

"You aren't dressed."

Kate looked down at herself. "Not yet. Just getting ready."

"Are you sick?"

"No." She thought of the pregnancy tests upstairs. She hadn't gotten as far as morning sickness, not yet. "I'm fine. Just running late, is all."

"Hmm." Sasha shouldered her bag and headed out of the room. She slammed the front door behind her without so much as a *bye.*

Undeterred, Kate opened the door, peering into the street to check the neighbors wouldn't see her in her robe.

"See you later!" she called. "Have a good day!"

Sasha didn't look round but gave her mother a dismissive wave. That was something, Kate thought. She closed the door, pondering on Sasha's behavior. Had she been more withdrawn lately, or was she always like that? Was Kate being paranoid? The girl was refusing to say anything about Robert or discuss anything that had happened with him. When Kate mentioned him, her daughter clammed up tight, answering her questions with *I'm fine* or *whatever.*

Did that make it more likely Sasha was hiding something, or less? Kate couldn't remember how it worked from her own teenage years. She'd had three noisy brothers and had pretty much been ignored at home, or that's how it had felt. She'd compensated by being an over-achiever.

She would have to keep her eye on her daughter, be ready for an opportunity when the girl might open up. Maybe one of the other moms might be able to talk to her. But Kate wasn't sure she wanted to trust another woman with the details of what had happened with Robert. She'd allowed him into their lives; she was culpable.

This was too hard, on her own.

Kate hurried upstairs and pulled a dark suit out of her closet. She ran a comb through her hair, barely glancing at the mirror next to her bed. She rushed back down to the kitchen table, gathered the files she'd been reading the night before—preparation for a court appearance today—and bundled them into her briefcase. Then she remembered the things under her pillow. Sasha would be home hours before her; she mustn't find them.

Kate clattered up the stairs, grabbed the sticks and

plunged them into her bag. She'd find a trashcan on the way to work. No need to keep them to be sure of what they meant.

~

The court appearance was unmemorable, a habitual burglar she'd defended before. Sometimes she'd got him off, sometimes not. This time was a not. Eighteen months in Travis County Jail; she wondered how long it would be before she was back here with him.

At lunchtime, she decided to take a walk. It was a crisp, sunny day. The sidewalks were thronged with people rushing between meetings, court hearings or lunch dates. She pulled her cellphone from her bag and sat on a bench.

"Hello, Sandra Wu speaking." Sandra was a junior colleague, a fourth-year associate to Kate's junior partner. They often worked together on cases which mixed family law, Sandra's specialty, with criminal law, Kate's.

"Hey Sandra, it's Kate."

"Kate? Are you coming back into the office?"

"Just getting some lunch. But look, Sandra, could I talk to you first?"

A pause. "Sure. I'll be here until three, then I've got a hearing. Hang by my office when you get back."

"I'd rather we talk outside the office, if you don't mind."

"Er, OK. Everything alright?"

"Nothing to worry about. Join me for a sandwich." She needed to make this sound casual; she had no idea if the office phones were recorded. "Meet me at Shoal Creek and 12th."

"Right by Thundercloud Subs."

"Exactly. Shall I get you something?"

"Why not. Ham on rye with pickles, please."

"No problem. See you in a moment."

"Let me just finish the case report I'm polishing off, then I'll be with you."

Kate headed for the sandwich bar and ordered Sandra's lunch. She wasn't hungry herself, but preferred not to consider why. She found an empty bench opposite the shop and sat down, clutching the brown bag on her lap. The street was quiet here, just the occasional passer-by, a car swishing past every ten seconds or so. She watched them, her breathing uneven.

"Hey." Sandra was hurrying, almost running. She'd need to be back at the office. Kate needed to get to the point.

Kate held out the bag. "Here."

Sandra sat next to Kate, who shuffled along the bench. She pulled her sandwich out and unwrapped it. "Thanks for this, I'm starving. Didn't get breakfast." She took a bite. "You not eating?"

"I already finished mine."

"Mmm." Sandra swallowed. "So what can I do for you? Something up at the office?"

"It's more personal than that." Kate dipped her head towards Sandra so she could lower her voice. Sandra gave her a puzzled frown but didn't pull back.

Kate swallowed. "Remember two years ago, when you were marching against Doe v Travis County?"

"I damn well do. Those bastards."

So Sandra hadn't lost her fire. That was good.

"Look," said Kate. "If I tell you something, will you keep it secret?"

Sandra's eyes widened. "You're pregnant."

Kate dropped her gaze and nodded. "Three weeks."

"Shit. Is it that handsome boyfriend of yours? The

doctor?" Her eyes widened. "Oh hell Kate, I'm sorry. That's none of my business."

Kate gave her a tight smile. "It is his, but he doesn't know. We split up."

"I'm sorry." Sandra swallowed. "That's rough."

Kate nodded again.

"You need me to cover for you, until you're ready to tell the partners?"

"No."

"What then?" Sandra's face fell. "Oh." She placed her sandwich in her lap.

Kate's mouth was dry. A loud group of students passed in front of them, laughing and shoving each other. Kate thought of Sasha and felt her stomach dip.

"I can't have it," she muttered.

Sandra stared at her for a moment. Then she licked her lips. "You're hoping I might know someone."

"You had friends in the campaign."

"I did." Sandra placed her brown bag on the floor and opened her purse. "I do." She rifled through her purse, muttering apologies as she did. She brought out two note-books, a collection of pens and a groaning makeup bag, and placed them on the bench between them. Then she drew out a business card.

"This has been hiding in here for years. I never knew if I'd need it." She held the card out to Kate. "Of course, it might not still be there."

Kate took it from her, her hand trembling. "Thank you."

Sandra put a hand on Kate's shoulder. "I'm sorry, Kate. Do you need me to drive you?"

"No thanks. This early on, it'll be straightforward." She looked from the card to her friend. "Assuming it's the same as it was when it was legal."

Sandra's face darkened. "Let's hope so."

Kate pushed her imagination to one side. She was only three weeks pregnant; it would be fine. She looked at the card again.

A name: *Sheila Higgins*. And a cell number. No information, no address. No *Dr*.

Kate looked back at Sandra. "It'll be fine. Thank you."

CHAPTER FOUR

GRACE PUT HER MUG ON THE COFFEE TABLE AND lifted her feet up next to it. Her ankles were swollen and her neck felt tight. Charlie had been giving her trouble tonight—a nightmare about puppies, of all things—and she was tired.

She reached out for the coffee, instantly regretting not putting it on the side table. After three attempts at grabbing it with her fingertips, she gave up. She didn't have the energy, and she could barely see the mug in the gloom. She'd stopped turning on the lights when she was alone, to save on the bills.

At least the remote was right next to her on the couch. She grabbed it and pointed it at the TV. A cop show. She flicked between channels—news, quizzes, more cop shows. She wanted something she could lose herself in.

She felt a twinge and dropped the remote. The baby was kicking. He didn't do that so much. She put her hand to her stomach and felt for where the movement had been. Did she want to seek out a tiny foot, or would she rather not? It would only make things worse.

Another twinge sent her toppling to one side. She hadn't had Braxton Hicks this bad with the other kids. She righted herself, pulling her back as straight as she could, and took a few deep breaths.

She thought of the doctor at her clinic yesterday. The way he'd avoided her eye after the ultrasound. The horrified look on his face when she'd asked about her options. "You do the best you can, Mrs Williams," was the stilted reply. "With God's help, you will find a way."

Find a way. She wondered if that doctor had three hungry kids at home, a husband on remand for a crime he didn't commit, and a job that was constantly under threat from school budget cuts. She wondered if he had to get up at 5.30am to get his kids' lunch ready and parcel them off on the school bus before walking to his own job because his car radiator was on the fritz again and he didn't have the money to get it fixed.

This baby would mean more struggle, more money, and more heartache. Especially now she knew it was going to be sick.

An incurable heart condition, they'd told her. It had shown up on the twenty week scan, a dark area in his heart that meant it wasn't getting the oxygen it needed. He might live for months, or weeks, or days. He might die before he was born. There was no surgery available that would save his tiny life.

She plunged her fist into her mouth to stifle a cry. That contraction was a big one. Not even Sissy had given her this much trouble, and she had been a livewire inside the womb.

Grace tried to stand up. She put her hand against the back of the couch and pushed, closing her eyes with the effort. She could feel sweat breaking out on her chin. Damn air conditioning broken again. It would stay that way until Linton was released.

With every ounce of effort she could summon, she pushed herself up and forward until she was standing between the couch and the coffee table.

What now?

She needed a hot water bottle. That would help. There was one at the back of a kitchen cupboard somewhere.

She picked up her feet and plodded towards the kitchen. From upstairs, she heard Charlie's voice—*Mom! I can't sleep*—and her stomach dipped. She couldn't do this.

At the threshold to the kitchen she paused to clutch the doorframe. Her legs were loose, her ankles swaying. The pains were coming at her now, clutching at her abdomen like a vice.

She knew this pain.

The baby was coming. She was twenty-one weeks pregnant; it wasn't her time. But maybe the poor mite knew what she did, and had decided to give up.

She crossed herself and muttered a prayer. She scanned the kitchen to find her cell phone; it was on the countertop next to the stove.

She didn't dare let go of the doorframe.

"Sissy," she breathed. Her daughter was only eight but she was a good girl, she'd been drilled by Grace and her husband Linton. In an emergency, call 911. Tell them your name and where you live. Don't hang up till they arrive. Despite what the authorities were currently doing to her husband, Grace had raised her kids to have respect. To trust.

She was glad they hadn't been there when that doctor had dismissed her yesterday. He'd looked at her like she was unfit to cross his threshold, like she was an abomination.

She couldn't call loud enough. Sissy was in her pink-painted bedroom, pretending to sleep. Watching videos on her big brother Boo's phone, most likely. They knew when Grace was tired, and sometimes they took advantage.

She stared at the phone then let go of the door frame. She took a step forward, then another one. She was doing it.

Then she fell. She felt her hip crash against the refrigerator, her arm slam into the tile below her.

A gust of air blew from her lips as she hit the ground. Something splashed red above her and a bowl of strawberries fell off the countertop, almost hitting her head. It smashed next to her, smearing the floor in red juices.

"Mom!"

She craned her neck to see behind her. Boo was standing at the foot of the stairs, his eyes wide. He was twelve years old and a good kid. Hard working, a baseball champ who'd been picked for county try-outs. He was going to get a scholarship, get himself out of this Godforsaken town with the shuttered stores and the closed-down businesses.

"Boo," she breathed. "Call 911."

"What is it Mom? Did you fall?"

Another contraction ricocheted through her. She bit down hard on her lip, not caring if it bled. "It's the baby, son. Make the call, will you?"

He nodded, his eyes wide and his cheeks pale. He grabbed the landline on its table at the bottom of the stairs and dialed, not taking his eyes off her for one moment.

"Uh, hello?"

She nodded, trying to encourage him. Her leg was bent beneath her, twisted at a strange angle. She could feel dampness between her legs. This baby had given up.

"Uh, my name is Boo Williams. I mean Robert Williams. I live at—"

She pushed out a smile as he told them their address. *Good boy*, she wanted to say to him. *That's it*. But her lungs were empty.

"It's my mom. She's pregnant." A pause. "Uh, 20 weeks, I think."

Twenty-one weeks, she thought. But it didn't matter.

"She's on the floor." He turned to her, his eyes huge. "Mom, can you get up?"

She pushed against her palm, which was in the pile of strawberries. "No," she whispered.

"No," he said into the phone. "She's real bad." His voice broke. She wanted to reach out to him, to hold him and tell him it would all be OK, that Mom would be looked after, that he and his sisters would be looked after. She frowned.

Sissy appeared behind her brother. "Mommy! What happened?" She ran to Grace and lay down next to her.

Grace looked into her daughter's eyes. "Sissy, honey," she said, trying to keep the panic out of her voice. "Go to Veronica next door. Ask if you can stay there tonight. All of you."

Sissy nodded. She paused to stroke her mom's cheek, then stood up. She ran out of the front door, leaving it to slam behind her. Boo was still on the phone; the ambulance people were keeping him on the line.

She heard the distant wail of sirens and let herself relax a little. She would be OK, and her kids would be safe. The baby was probably dead already, but from what the doctor had told her, it wouldn't have lasted more than a few weeks anyway. Maybe it was a kindness.

She closed her eyes and sank into unconsciousness as the sirens approached.

CHAPTER FIVE

Beef Stroganov was Sasha's favorite. Kate pushed the meat around the pan, her stomach fluttering as she waited for the sound of the front door.

At last, it opened. She poked her head round the kitchen door.

"Hey, honey. Good study group?"

Sasha had one foot on the bottom stair. Her jacket was on the floor at her feet. Kate said nothing.

"Fine."

"I'm cooking Stroganov."

"Cool."

Sasha turned away and hurried up the stairs. Kate tried to pull her heart up from the pit of her stomach.

A half hour later, the meal was ready. Kate rearranged the table in the kitchen, wanting to make it nice but not too nice.

She climbed the stairs and knocked on her daughter's door. She entered, not waiting for a response.

"Dinner's ready."

"Give me a minute."

"Don't be too long. It'll go cold."

A roll of the eyes. "I know."

Kate slid back downstairs, watching Sasha's door. She plated up the food and placed it on the table. She poured herself a small glass of wine and some juice for Sasha.

She moved her food around the plate, not wanting to finish before Sasha arrived.

Just as she was about to go back up, she heard footsteps on the stairs. She forced herself to breathe again.

"What's the occasion?"

"No occasion. Just thought I'd make something nice."

"You normally make this for my birthday. That's not for six months."

"Think of this as a half-birthday, then."

"That would be in ten days."

Kate nodded. She watched Sasha's expression pick up as she ate; this was still her favorite, then.

"How's school?"

"Fine. The usual."

"Any excitement?"

"Like what?" Sasha drained her juice and went to the fridge for more.

"I don't know. New friends, anything interesting you've learned."

"Nope. Same old, same old."

Kate smiled. "Want some more?"

Sasha looked up, her face momentarily that of the little girl who had begged for this meal on her sixth birthday. "There's more?"

"Sure." She held her hand out to take Sasha's plate. She went to the stove and piled more food onto it, then placed it in front of her daughter, who started eating as if she hadn't been fed for days.

Kate took a breath. "Robert won't be coming back, you know."

"OK."

"I thought you might be pleased."

A shrug. "You liked him."

"That was before I saw what he was doing to you."

Sasha put down her fork. "It was nothing, Mom."

"Nothing? You sure?"

"I'm sure. Stop working yourself up about it."

"Did he touch you like that before?"

Another shrug. Kate lowered her voice. "You can tell me, sweetie."

Sasha shook her head. "Just once. Two days earlier. He put his hand on my knee at dinner."

Kate almost dropped her fork. "At dinner?"

A nod. Sasha's cheeks were bright red.

"Was I there?"

"You were working late."

Kate felt herself crumple. She'd stayed out late and left her daughter in the care of a monster.

"What did you do? When he touched your knee."

"I moved away."

"And then what did he do?"

"Mom. I don't want to talk about it."

"Just this once. Tell me what he did, and I'll never bother you about it again."

Silence.

"I promise."

Sasha put down her fork; she'd stopped halfway through her second helping. "He laughed, and then he carried on eating. He didn't try it again."

"But he was stroking your cheek, two days later. I saw how he had you cornered."

"I wasn't exactly cornered, Mom."

"Did he hurt you? Did he say anything inappropriate?"

"He was silent. Both times. He looked at me with these dumb eyes like some eighth-grade kid with a crush."

Kate felt a shiver run across her skin. "Anything else you want to tell me?"

"No. He touched me, just the twice. I could have stopped him. Mom. You didn't have to come barging in."

"I'm glad I did."

"Whatever."

Sasha stood up. She pushed her chair in and headed for the door.

"You haven't finished your dinner," Kate said, pushing the tremor out of her voice.

"I'm not hungry."

CHAPTER SIX

GRACE WOKE TO FIND HERSELF STARING AT A flickering fluorescent tube in the center of a gray-stained ceiling about four feet above her head.

She pulled her hand up to rub her eyes and frowned; something was tugging at it. She looked down to see a canula attached to the back of her wrist.

She felt it, tempted to tug it out, then thought better of it. There was a dull pain where the tube had snagged on her skin as she'd moved.

She pulled herself up in the bed and shuffled against the scratchy pillows. She was in a hospital ward. A set of drawn curtains hid the occupant of the bed opposite. On her right, a young white woman was sleeping, her face turned towards Grace. Her eyes were ringed with red and her cheeks were almost translucent. Grace watched her for a moment then turned away, feeling like a voyeur.

In the bed to her left was a woman of about Grace's age, reading a magazine. The biggest bouquet of flowers Grace had ever seen stood on her nightstand: carnations and roses. She turned to Grace and smiled.

"Hello."

"Hello," Grace replied. There was a dull ache in her stomach, and she could feel a thick sanitary pad inside her underwear. "What time is it?"

The woman glanced at her watch. "It's almost three in the afternoon. Tuesday. You've been out for a while."

Grace shivered. "How long?"

The woman placed her magazine on her lap. Her face was heavily lined, but full of light. "Since they brought you here about midnight."

"Midnight. Where are my kids?"

The woman's smile dropped. "I'm sorry, honey. I ain't seen no kids. Maybe they're with family?"

Would the kids have had the sense to ring their Aunt Sylvia? Would her sister have been home? Then she remembered telling Sissy to go to Veronica next door. Vee would take care of them.

She pulled the sheet up over her chest. She was wearing a rough cotton gown, hospital issue. She checked the nightstand; there was nothing of her own.

"You OK?" The woman looked worried.

"I'll be fine. Just need to see my kids, is all."

"Mine were in here for two hours today. Wore me out." She chuckled. "Did me good to hold them, though."

Grace wondered why the other woman was here. It wouldn't do to pry.

"Have the doctors said anything about me? You overheard anything?"

"Oh, I'm sorry. They have been checking you, but I closed my ears. Didn't want to snoop."

"I understand."

"There's one headed this way now, you could grab him."

Grace turned to see a young white doctor striding across

the ward. There were at least twelve beds, all women, most black, one white, a few Latina. They were all quiet, except for one woman in the far corner who was sobbing like she might never stop. Grace raised her hand to catch the doctor's attention, but he was looking at her anyway.

"Good luck," the woman with the flowers whispered.

Grace swallowed as she waited. The ache in her stomach was growing, reminding her of the debilitating periods she'd suffered as a girl.

"Ms Williams." The doctor stopped at her bed and grabbed the chart which hung over its foot. He flipped through the pages, not looking her in the eye.

"Mrs," she corrected him.

"Mrs Williams. I apologize."

"What happened to me?" She lowered her voice. "The baby?"

The doctor pulled the curtains around her bed. She waited, wishing he would hurry.

"I'm Doctor Pardoe," he said. "I work with Doctor LeRange. He's your consultant."

She didn't care who was what. "Tell me about my baby, please."

His face darkened. "I'm sorry, Mrs Williams. The baby didn't make it."

The pain in her stomach clutched at her. She clenched her fists. "How?"

"We aren't sure, Mrs Williams. We still need to get to the bottom of things."

"What do you mean, bottom of things?"

He dropped his gaze. "People are looking at your records, at the evidence from the paramedics. We still aren't sure."

"What *evidence?*"

"I'm sorry. When Doctor LeRange comes back on shift, I'll send him to you. He'll be much better at explaining things than me." He still wasn't looking her in the eye.

"When will you let me go home? When can I see my kids?"

"That I can't say. Not until... well, not until you're all better. And we're ready to let you go."

He gave her a curt nod and pulled back, the curtains parting around him. She opened her mouth to frame another question, but he was gone.

"Hello?" she called. "Come back!"

The doctor reappeared. This time he was flushed.

"We have a development, Mrs Williams."

"What kind of development?"

"Er..." He scratched his nose. "You have visitors."

She felt the tension fall away. "My kids. Are they with my neighbor, or my sister?"

He shook his head.

"It's not your family, Mrs Williams."

"Who, then?"

The doctor cleared his throat. "It's the police, Mrs Williams. They need to talk to you."

CHAPTER SEVEN

SHEILA HIGGINS WAS A WOMAN OF ABOUT FIFTY WITH a mop of unruly red hair and a lopsided smile. She looked uneasy as she ushered Kate into her cramped consulting room. Books lined the walls, papers were strewn on the desk and empty mugs littered the surfaces.

Kate glanced back into the waiting room, wondering if the young woman at reception knew why she was here. The space was full of patients, mainly women, a couple of men sitting next to their partners. Were at least some of them here for the same reason? Or was this an everyday above-board gynecologist's office?

Dr Higgins—she was a medical doctor, thank God—closed the door and waved in the direction of a desk and two chairs. Kate's rocked when she sat down, its leather upholstery old and worn.

Dr Higgins smiled and glanced at the door. She sat opposite Kate and steepled her fingertips together, elbows on the desk. She paused to push a mug of what looked like cold coffee to one side. She licked her lips then lowered her hands on to the wood.

"So," she said. "How many weeks?"

Kate blinked; she hadn't been expecting to get to the point this quickly. "Just six, almost seven."

"That's good."

Kate nodded. She'd gone to an Internet cafe and done some research, found some sites from before Doe v Travis County. Some Canadian sites too. It seemed that if you had the money you could travel to Canada and have it done there. Kate did have the money, but she didn't want to wait. If she could get this done by a real doctor, then it would be no different from when her friend Lola had done the same back when they were in college.

Except Lola hadn't been breaking the law. And Kate was a criminal lawyer.

"I need to see an ultrasound first," Dr Higgins said. "Establish the gestation period. If you took the pills I'm going to give you too late, it could cause problems."

"That's fine."

"I've got you on my appointment sheet as an initial fertility consult. Sorry. But I have to put something down in the file. It's not unusual to give a woman an ultrasound when we suspect uterine abnormalities that might have an impact on ability to conceive."

"Don't I need to have the father with me for fertility treatment?"

"Yes. For the treatment itself. As you probably know, single women are no longer permitted fertility assistance. But for the initial consults and the diagnosis, you don't need to bring anyone." She paused. "Is there a man on the scene?"

"No."

"That's good. Less complicated. The fewer people you tell about this, the better."

"I understand."

The doctor stood up. "Right." She grabbed a pack of latex gloves. "Let's get you up onto the bed and take a look, huh?"

Kate lay on the gurney under the window and lifted her shirt, thinking of when she had done this with Sasha. She wondered what Sasha would think about this, if she were ever to tell her. Her daughter still hadn't spoken about Robert. Kate's fear was that he had touched her before. She'd remembered conversations, the way they were at the dinner table together. Sasha had been withdrawn and cagey for weeks, and had refused to look Robert in the eye. Kate had just assumed it was the upheaval of having a new boyfriend around the place.

"I'm sorry," said the doctor. "We have to do this internally, at this stage."

"Oh."

"I'll draw this curtain for you, then you tell me when you're ready."

Kate removed her panties and placed them under her purse, feeling inexplicably modest. She could hear the doctor moving around on the other side of the curtain. She lay back again, shuffling to get comfortable. There was a sheet of paper; she placed it over her abdomen.

"Ready."

The doctor smiled as she pulled the curtain. "Wonderful. Now, you let me know if I hurt you at all. OK?"

"OK."

"Right. I assume you don't want to see?"

"No thanks."

"That's one of the advantages of doing it this way." The doctor poured jelly on the ultrasound wand and inserted it in Kate's vagina, her eyes on the screen between them that faced away from Kate. Kate drew in breath while the doctor continued talking. "In the old days, I would have had to force you to look. Informed consent. As if you were too dumb to understand what you were doing."

Kate nodded. She didn't want to chat. She wanted to get on with this, then go home to her daughter. The sky was darkening outside. A storm was brewing.

The doctor withdrew the wand and pressed a button on the screen. She grabbed a tissue and wiped the jelly off the wand. She looked at Kate.

"Spot on. Seven weeks."

"OK. What now?"

"Get yourself dressed and I'll give you the drugs." She pushed the curtain to one side and disappeared.

When Kate emerged and sat down again, the doctor was pulling an unmarked box out of a safe in the wall behind her. Kate stared at it.

"Er, where do you get them?" she asked.

"The less you know, the better." Dr Higgins's smile dropped. "Alright?"

"Alright." She would have to trust this woman. Either that, or make the trip to Canada with its week-long waiting process.

"OK. So. I need you to take this pill now." She held out a plastic cup with a single pill in it, and a cup of water. "Then the other pill you take at home. Wait between twelve and twenty-four hours before taking it. Once you've taken this one, I recommend going straight home. You'll get cramping in the next few hours, and then more when you take the second pill."

Kate eyed the little yellow pill then closed her eyes and placed it on her tongue. She took a swig of the water and swallowed.

She put the other pill in her purse, resolving to hide it as soon as she got home. Sasha sometimes went in her purse looking for stationery.

The doctor stood up, her hand outstretched. "Good luck. Tracey will take your payment on the way out."

Kate had forgotten about that part of the transaction. She had a thousand dollars in her purse, in cash. She'd told the bank she was having her kitchen renovated.

"Thank you," she said, backing towards the door. But the doctor had her head bent toward a computer monitor, checking the details of her next client no doubt.

Kate shuffled toward the reception desk, eyeing the other patients. She withdrew the envelope from her purse and slid it across the counter.

"Thank you," she said.

The young woman gave her a wary look. "Thank you." She didn't look at the envelope, but instead slid it into an open drawer. Kate wondered what happened to women who didn't hand over the correct amount. What recourse would this doctor possibly have? Or was it all done on trust?

She pushed out in to the parking lot. Sure enough, clouds were gathering on the horizon, the sky the color of a bruise. The flower-dotted shrubs that flanked the parking lot were plunged into shade. She hurried to her car and dove into the driver's seat.

She opened her purse and pulled out the unmarked box. Misoprostol. The drug which had routinely been given to women seeking an early abortion prior to Doe. She'd assumed it would always be available. But now here she was, slipping envelopes of money into the hands of doctors who were able to obtain it illegally.

She heard engine noise behind her and turned.

A car behind blocked her way, one of two identical

white cars between her and the clinic. They were both squad cars. Austin PD.

She held her breath, watching in her rear-view mirror. She felt for the box again, wondering what to do.

Clinics like this were getting raided every couple months. At first it had been weekly, until they'd either disappeared or learned to avoid suspicion. With that many police cars lined up behind her, she knew why they were here.

Would they question every woman here, demand to search their bags?

If they had reasonable cause, they could treat every woman in this clinic and its vicinity as suspects. The envelope she had handed over gave them enough. As did the contents of that safe.

And the contents of her purse.

She looked toward the street. If she left her car, could she walk away? Could she hail a cab? Her car would still be here. And her name, on file.

She let out a long breath and looked in the mirror again. There was no one around; the cars were still there, but their occupants were inside.

It was tempting.

It was dumb.

She had a bottle of water in the glove locker. She grabbed it and took the pill out of its packet, glancing in her rear-view mirror as she did so. At least twelve hours, the doctor had said. She had no idea if that was to ensure it worked properly, or for Kate's own safety.

She took a deep breath and swallowed the pill. She crumpled the unmarked box in the bottom of her purse and opened the car door, heading back to the clinic.

CHAPTER EIGHT

Cindee looked at the doctor through lowered lashes as she entered the consulting room. This wasn't her first time ; she'd been here already, listening to the woman trying to be nice to her.

She wished she wouldn't. Cindee didn't want people to be nice to her.

"Morning, Cindee. Take a seat."

She did as she was told, like she always did. Whatever they claimed Cindee had done, she would never make trouble. That was the way she'd been raised. A good girl.

At least, until she'd tried to kill her unborn baby. She'd deserved to be caught. She even deserved to carry this baby —*his* baby—to term, and face whatever that meant.

The chair was hard, one leg too short. She tensed her stomach and clenched her toes inside the flimsy prison-issue shoes to keep from toppling. She placed her hands in her lap and looked down at them.

"Do you know why you're here today?"

She nodded. An examination, the doctor had told her. At least it was the same doctor, the *call me Maya* one. As if she'd ever do that. Her mother would go crazy if she heard Cindee talking to a doctor like that.

"That's good. But I need to remind you anyway. I have to give you an examination, to see how you and your baby are doing. You're eighteen weeks pregnant, is that correct?"

Cindee nodded, wiping her cheek. If that was what they told her, it must be correct. She was trying not to count.

"Fine. So I'm going to feel your stomach, find out which way the baby is lying if I can. And I'm going to take some measurements. In a couple of weeks, when you're twenty weeks gone, I'll give you an ultrasound. But I see no reason to do that today."

Cindee shrugged. What would her mom say, if she saw her being so rude to the doctor. *Buck up your ideas, girl*, is what. But Mom was a long way away now. The last time Cindee had seen her had been the first day of her trial, when her mother had sat in the crowd, her eyes fixed ahead, her face still. She'd listened to the evidence that first day, the details of how Cindee had gotten pregnant. She hadn't come back the second day.

"OK. I'll be gentle, Cindee. I know this is hard for you. I'll do my best to make it as comfortable as possible."

Cindee raised her head to look at the doctor. She had a kind face, large brown eyes and smooth skin with a single mole—beauty mark, her mom would say—on her left cheek. She wore perfectly applied pink lipstick and a dark brown eyeshadow that complemented her skin color. She meant well. But Cindee didn't want her kindness.

The doctor's smile widened and Cindee dropped her gaze. She twisted her hands together in her lap. She thought of the woman at the clinic who'd smiled at her just like this as she'd bustled out of her office. There'd been no smiles when the cops arrived though. When the doctor was rushing Cindee and her sister Size along corridors, helping them get away. She'd shoved them out of a fire door, only for them to be confronted by more cops outside.

"Let's get you up on the couch, hey?"

Cindee looked around to see a thin couch by the wall behind her. There was a roll of paper at the end of it, like a huge roll of lavatory paper.

Slowly she pushed herself out of the chair, ignoring a movement inside her.

The doctor held a hand out as if wanting to help her. "You get yourself ready and I'll be right with you."

Cindee frowned.

The doctor shrugged. "Just lie back and pull up your t-shirt. Pull your pants down, just a little, to expose your bump."

The doctor pulled the curtain closed between them. Cindee pulled up the prison-issue white t-shirt and pulled down her waistband, just as she'd been told.

"Ready yet?"

"Uh-huh."

The doctor swished the curtain aside, hands outstretched. Cindee swallowed hard.

The doctor rubbed gel over her hands as Cindee looked up at the ceiling, listening to the doctor preparing herself. She closed her eyes and then opened them again.

There was a spider in the corner, weaving its web. She watched it, hoping that would distract her.

She felt the doctor's hand on her stomach and flinched.

"I'm sorry, was that a surprise?"

Cindee shrugged. The paper beneath her crinkled against her shoulders.

"I'll warn you next time."

Cindee looked at the ceiling again. The spider had gone, its web empty in the corner. She scanned the ceiling, hoping it wasn't about to land on her.

"Alright, here goes. I'm about to put both hands on your stomach."

Cindee nodded, her eyes sharp. She felt two hands land on her flesh and was surprised by how warm they were.

"Now, I'm going to move my hands across your stomach. I'll have to put some pressure on."

Cindee blinked. She let out a thin breath then closed her eyes.

The doctor moved her hands across the top of Cindee's abdomen, twisting them as she went. Cindee felt her skin tighten and her breathing accelerate. She muttered a prayer.

"What was that? Everything OK?" The doctor stopped moving her hands.

"Yes. Sorry."

"It's alright. Just tell me if you need me to stop."

Cindee sniffed and closed her eyes again. Her eyelids were bright red.

The doctor moved her hands; downwards this time. Cindee clenched her fists, feeling her fingernails biting into the flesh of her palms.

This was what she'd done when he'd visited her room. Find another sensation, however painful, anything to shift her focus elsewhere. She'd taken to hiding a blade under her pillow, so she could twist it into her palm when he wasn't looking. It had never occurred to her to use it against him.

The doctor twisted a hand and prodded the base of Cindee's abdomen with her thumb.

"No."

The movement stopped. "Cindee? Am I hurting you?"

Cindee didn't know she'd spoken aloud. She took a breath. "No. You're not." She bit down on her bottom lip.

The doctor put a reassuring hand on her wrist, but it just made Cindee's whole arm tense up. *Move it*, she thought. *Take it away.*

She squeezed her eyes shut as the doctor took her hand off her arm. She forced herself to breathe. There were two hands on her abdomen now; one at the top and one at the bottom. She pulled her focus away from it to her palms, into which she was drilling her fingernails. *Breathe*, she told herself. She could do this.

She felt something brush her skin, something cold and flat. She gasped.

"Sorry. That's my tape measure. I'm measuring the fundal height."

Cindee had no idea what that meant. She felt a tear make its way down the side of her face and into her hair.

The doctor pulled the tape taut and pushed her fingertips into the top and bottom of Cindee's abdomen. Cindee could feel her breathing coming fast now. He'd done this. He'd traced a line down her stomach with his fingers, all the way from her small breasts to her pubic hair. She'd cried silently as he did it, waiting for what came next.

She let out a loud sob and threw her hands down to her stomach. She felt them slap the doctor's hands. She screamed.

"Cindee? I'm sorry."

She let out a guttural sound, something she could imagine an animal making. She felt herself jumping off the high couch and throwing herself to the floor. She wasn't sure if she'd moved deliberately, or if she was being controlled by a force outside her. Had she been possessed?

She scuttled into the corner of the room, picturing the

spider above her head. She was directly below its web, curled into the place where the walls met. She pulled up her knees and folded her arms around them.

The doctor was in front of her, her shadow blocking out the fluorescent tube.

"Cindee, I'm so sorry. I'll stop now. We can continue another day."

Another day? Cindee couldn't go through this another day. She pulled her knees in tighter and sobbed into them, rubbing her face into the hard bone of her kneecaps. She wished she had a knife she could drill into her palm, or plunge into her heart.

"No!" She cried. "No."

The doctor bent to her. She put a hand out but didn't touch Cindee. "We need to get you back to your cell. I have another appointment in a few minutes. I'll help you, make sure no one knows."

Cindee looked up at her. She blinked a few times to bring the woman's face into focus. This was the doctor she'd met twice now, a woman with a kind, flushed face and wide eyes. It wasn't her father.

She nodded. "Take me back," she whispered.

CHAPTER NINE

GRACE WAITED FOR THE DRAPES TO PART AGAIN, HER skin bristling. Was this something to do with Linton? Had his court date been brought forward? And how had the cops found her here?

At last a hand appeared between the drapes and pulled them to one side. It was a woman, a young black woman who reminded Grace of her niece, Kylene. A man followed her: white, fat, balding.

She rearranged herself in the bed, pulling the sheet up higher. She wished she'd asked for her own nightclothes. She blinked at them, waiting for them to speak first.

"Are you Grace Williams?" the man asked. He was out of breath, his chest rising and falling noticeably.

"Well yes. Of course I am." She tried to keep her voice steady.

He nodded. "We're here to talk to you about your miscarriage."

She blinked back a tear. Why did they care about her poor dead baby? She said nothing, waiting.

The woman attempted a smile. "I'm Detective Morrison. This is Detective Nowak. We're from the Dallas police. We're investigating a suspected homicide."

"Homicide?" She felt her heart lurch in her ribcage. "Who?"

The woman lowered her eyes then raised them again. Grace felt her chest hollow out. "Whose homicide?" she repeated. "Not my husband?"

The woman—Detective Morrison—shook her head. She was no more than thirty years old, and slender. She wore a gray trouser suit with a pink shirt beneath. She dragged a chair closer to the bed. Grace wondered if her neighbor was listening in from the next bed.

"Mrs Williams, can you tell us about the circumstances under which you lost your baby?"

"I don't understand. Who's been killed? Tell me. You're scaring me."

"We believe your baby was killed," the woman said. Her voice was low.

"Killed? What do you mean, killed?" Her mind went back to the previous night, the pains coming on when she was getting ready for bed. "I don't know what you're talking about."

The woman took a deep breath. "Mrs Williams. Grace. The doctors tell us that your baby had an abnormality."

A twitch ran through Grace's cheek. "A heart condition. Yes."

"And that you didn't want to give birth to a child that would be born deformed."

"What makes you—?"

"Did you ask Dr Eliot Sims about an abortion, Mrs Williams?" Detective Nowak's voice was rough; he was a smoker.

"Did I what? No. I don't know what you're talking about."

The man approached the bed. "Your baby was twenty-two weeks old."

"Twenty-one," Grace corrected him.

"Twenty-one. Are you aware that killing a viable fetus constitutes homicide in the state of Texas?"

"I didn't kill no one."

"Your baby." The young woman was talking now. She was trying to look concerned, to make like she cared. Grace wanted to spit on her. "It was at legal viability. We have reason to believe you deliberately tried to abort the child yourself. Which, as my colleague has said, is homicide."

"I had a miscarriage. I didn't try to kill anyone. Where are my children? Two boys and a girl. I haven't seen them yet. They'll be missing me."

Her breathing was coming shallow and rapid, and she could feel her head lightening. She'd felt like this last night, before she'd passed out on the kitchen floor.

"Where's the doctor?" she cried. "He can tell you. They'll have examined me."

"We have a statement from your obstetrician Dr Sims. He says you asked him if you could get an abortion."

"I did no such thing! I asked what my options were. That's all."

The cops eyed each other across the bed. The man nodded at the woman.

The woman turned to Grace. She wouldn't meet her eye.

"Grace Williams, I'm arresting you on suspicion of unlawful killing of a viable fetus. You have the right to remain silent. Anything you say can and will be used against you..."

CHAPTER TEN

KATE OPENED THE DOORS TO THE CLINIC. SHE STRODE in, her best lawyer expression on her face. Whatever she did, she couldn't escape this situation. But she could help the woman who not more than a half-hour ago had helped her.

Two uniformed cops stood either side. Beyond them, three more were turning over the reception area. Two men in crumpled suits—one blue, one gray—were sifting through files, talking to each other. There was no sign of the clinic staff, or any remaining patients. Kate wondered where they had gone; there must be a back door. Either that, or she hadn't spotted the exodus before her car had been blocked in by the cops.

"Excuse me, Ma'am. You can't come in here," one of the unformed cops at the door told her.

"I'm a lawyer. Is this a legal search?"

"Of course it's a legal search. Who do you think we are, the Keystone Cops?"

"Who's under suspicion here, and of what?"

"I don't think that's any of your business."

She hesitated. "Just tell me you have a warrant."

He stiffened and gestured toward one of the detectives. She strode toward him, doing everything she could to project poise. She could feel the faintest of aches in her abdomen, like the early twinges of a period coming on.

"My name is Kate Mitchell," she said as she pulled a business card from her inside pocket. "I'm from White, Petersik and Abad, criminal lawyers. Do you have a warrant to search these premises?"

"Kate Mitchell?" The detective replied. He had a faint scar running from his left ear across his cheek.

"That's what I said. Do you have a warrant?"

"Your name is in here."

She felt her chest tighten. "That's irrelevant. Show me your warrant."

He turned a computer monitor to face her. "That your name?"

"Yes. I'm a patient here."

"Been coming here a while?"

"Today was my first time."

"Hmm."

"What's going on?" Doctor Higgins emerged from a door behind the reception desk. Her jacket was crooked and her hair even more disheveled.

"Dr Higgins," said Kate. "Did they show you a warrant? They can't just push their way in here and destroy your property."

"They had a warrant." The doctor glanced at the cop.

Kate licked her lips. "Have they read you your Miranda rights?"

"I thought that was only if they arrested me."

Kate turned to the cop. "Sergeant—?"

"Sergeant Malone," he replied.

"Sergeant Malone, is Dr Higgins free to leave the premises?"

"Not until we've questioned her."

"Then you're detaining her. Read her her rights, or it will be an unlawful arrest."

He sighed. The doctor had paled. She looked at Kate as if blaming her for all this.

"Sheila Higgins, you have the right to remain silent. Anything you say can and will be used against you in a court of law. You have the right to an attorney. If you cannot afford an attorney, one will be provided for you." He garbled the words, barely looking the doctor in the eye.

"Do you have a lawyer?" Kate asked.

The doctor nodded. "Derek Lawson, at Myers and Fitch."

"He's good. You should call him."

"Hang on a sec," interrupted Sergeant Malone. "It doesn't work like that."

"It does and you know it," said Kate. "She's entitled to a phone call to her attorney. I suggest you let her make it here, save your phone bill at the station."

He twisted his lips at her. "Irritating bitch, aren't you?"

She flinched. "Just doing my job."

He bent to listen to one of the uniformed cops, who was whispering in his ear. A smile broke across his gray face.

"I have news for you, Ms Mitchell."

She squared her shoulders. She could feel the drugs taking effect now, the cramps beginning.

"Yes?" she said, pushing calm into her voice.

"The doctor here isn't the only one we need to

Miranda. I'm arresting you on suspicion of obtaining an illegal abortion. You need me to repeat it all for you?"

She glared at him. "Go on." Anything to annoy him.

The officer brought handcuffs out of his pocket and fastened them on Kate's wrist. She tried to ignore the pain in her abdomen as she listened to the charges against her.

CHAPTER ELEVEN

Maya hadn't spoken to anyone about Cindee's reaction to being touched the previous week. Instead, she'd noted only what measurements she'd managed to take.

In the meantime she'd been given a new patient: Grace, a thirty-four year-old woman who'd given herself a third-term abortion. At least, that's what she was charged with. Maya found it hard to believe that this gentle woman with her singsong voice would deliberately kill a baby that was almost ready to be born, even if the baby was going to be born severely ill.

Part of her job was to find evidence. She had to find signs of trauma inside Grace's body, signs Grace had used any kind of instrument to bring about the abortion. The admitting doctor had already sent off a blood sample when Grace had been brought to the prison, and the results of that would be back anytime between a week and a month from now. The system ground along at its own pace.

Today was Grace's second consultation. Tuesday had been the customary initial assessment, where Maya asked questions and the woman, usually, refused to answer. Today was a physical exam.

This was her first appointment of the day and Grace was already waiting outside Maya's office. A CO stood next to her, not speaking.

"Good morning, Grace. Good to see you."

"Morning, Doctor."

"Call me Maya. Please."

The guard frowned at Maya but she ignored him.

"Come in." She turned to the guard. "Thank you." He grunted and shuffled away. He smelled of cigarettes and mint-flavored gum.

Grace walked into the room, Maya watching her move. She looked as if she was in pain; her back was bent and she wasn't properly picking up her feet. Maya pulled out a chair.

"Take a seat."

"Thank you."

Maya threw Grace an encouraging smile and sat behind her desk. She pulled the chair out a little so they weren't blocked by the desk between them.

"How are you feeling today?" She opened Grace's file on her laptop. Grace was a high school teacher and mother to three children.

"Not so bad. Tired."

"I can imagine. So I have the results from the exam you had when you arrived."

"Oh."

"You're healing nicely. You don't have any infection."

"Good. What about the other thing?"

"I'm sorry, I can't talk to you about that. Your lawyer will be able to discuss any findings with you."

Grace's shoulders slumped. Maya wanted to tell her

that what she'd found had been inconclusive; that there was scarring in Maya's vagina and that it could have been caused by an instrument used to bring on an abortion, but that most probably it was the speculum used by the doctors at the ER. The inside of a woman's body was hardly a clean crime scene.

"I wanted to ask you a favor."

Grace turned her face to Maya for the first time. It was smooth and high-cheeked; not as worn as Maya's would have been if she'd had Grace's life. "A favor?"

"Yes. I have another patient."

"Prisoner."

"Patient. She's young, very young. She won't talk about her life before she came here but I think she's had a rough time."

Grace shrugged. *They've all had a rough time*, thought Maya.

"You're a high school teacher, right?"

"Used to be."

"I thought maybe you could help her. Talk to her. "

"Why me?"

"Like you say, you used to be a teacher. I imagine you're good at talking to teenagers. Better than me, anyway." Maya was single; no man, no kids.

"I don't think it's a good idea," said Grace.

"Why not? It gives you something to do here, and might help a girl in distress."

Grace shook her head. "I don't want to get attached to anyone. I'll have my trial, and then I'll be going home." She straightened her back; there was an almost imperceptible twitch in her cheek.

Maya heard movement in the corridor outside; was her next appointment here already? "It won't take long. I'm not asking you to make lifelong friends with the girl. But you could help her. I know you could."

"Isn't that *your* job?"

"She won't talk to me. I've tried."

"Maybe you haven't tried hard enough."

"Look Grace, take it or leave it. I'm offering you some purpose here. And a chance to help make a difference for this young girl. I'm not saying investigate her. You don't have to find out what happened to her. And you certainly don't need to report back to me. But I think you have the experience to help her, and I think she could use some help."

Grace eyed Maya. "I think you're being cruel."

Maya leaned back. "I'm trying to help." She hoped Grace didn't talk to the COs like this.

"You're interfering. You're trying to keep me busy, so I don't dwell on what the venerable state of Texas has done to me. When I get out of here, this poor girl will be deprived of a relationship you want to set her up with."

"I assure you my motives are a lot less complex than you seem to think."

A shrug. "Kids can get attached. Even at sixteen. Especially at sixteen. It wouldn't be fair on her."

"What if I told you I had concerns she might be suicidal?"

Grace gave her a look of disapproval. "I imagine the prison has procedures for that."

"I don't want to get her into trouble with the COs."

"So you'd let her kill herself?"

"No." Maya dragged her hand through her hair. "Look, maybe I'm exaggerating. But I think she could use your help."

"You really are a determined lady."

"I'm a doctor. I want to see my patients get better. I have no idea what's happened to Cindee, and I don't expect you to go prying. I just believe a friendly face would be a big help to her."

Grace sighed. "A friendly face."

"Yes."

"You think this is a friendly face?" Grace held a finger up to point to her own face. She looked tired and drawn.

"You have experience. I don't."

Grace gazed at her, her face impassive. "You've got a lot to learn."

CHAPTER TWELVE

HE MEANS WELL, THOUGHT KATE, WATCHING HER colleague Josh run her defense. It was sensible to have a male lawyer. It was equally sensible not to defend herself; even the most experienced criminal attorney would struggle with their own case.

But that didn't make it any easier. Josh was a competent attorney, a good one even. But he didn't have the bite she did.

This was her sentencing hearing; she'd pled guilty, knowing the evidence was stacked against her. She'd been in the parking lot of the clinic; her name was on the database; the empty pill packet found in her car matched the packets in the doctor's safe. And those all held pills which the State had analyzed and shown to be Misoprostol, the drug which brought on an abortion. She'd suffered from cramping as she'd been arrested, and at the police station they'd found blood in her underwear. It was all stacked against her.

"Sir, you've seen the file on my client," Josh said, standing in front of Judge Kusak. The courtroom was quiet;

just her and Josh, the Assistant DA on the other side, and the judge. No one was here to witness it, because she hadn't told anyone she would be here.

She would get a fine, a slap on the wrist. Maybe she'd be prevented from practicing law for a few months. She could hide that from Sasha; when Julian had left her, she'd learned to save her money when she could, and had a few months' worth of salary in the bank. They could tighten their belts.

The most important thing was for this not to become public. The kind of client who was happy to hire a convicted felon as their criminal lawyer was not the kind of client she wanted.

"Ms Mitchell is a model citizen," Josh continued. "She has not been arrested before, let alone charged or convicted. She's only had two parking tickets in fifteen years of driving. She's the mother to a teenage daughter and a key member of the White, Petersik and Abad law practice."

"*Your* law practice," interrupted the Assistant DA. "I don't see what her invaluableness to your firm has to do with her sentencing."

Josh continued to look at the judge "My point is that Kate Mitchell has people depending on her. Her husband left her three years ago to bring up their daughter alone. She holds down a good job and provides for her family. She's never been in trouble before. And the abortion she sought was at just seven weeks of pregnancy. I would like to draw the court's attention to McGraw vs Bern, in which the court ruled that an abortion in the first trimester should receive the minimum sentence allowed for under the law, which is a fine and two weeks' community service."

The judge waved a hand in dismissal. "That was in

Ohio," he said. "Lower court. You shouldn't be wasting my time with that sort of nonsense, son."

Josh blinked a few times, derailed by the *son*. He was only three years younger than Kate but his round face and thin beard made him look ten years younger. *Hold it together*, she thought.

"I apologize, sir," Josh replied. "In that case I would like to refer you to Putnam vs Trey, heard in this very state on 13 November last year.'

"I know all about Putnam. You don't need to remind me of that one."

He was right, thought Kate. Judge Kusak had had to recuse himself from the case after it had been revealed he knew the parents of the woman involved.

The judge scratched his nose. "The doctor—if you can call her that—who ran the clinic has been given the maximum sentence. Your client was involved in the same incident. They were conspirators in procuring an illegal abortion for your client."

"My client did not take part in any conspiracy to provide abortions. She met the clinic director just the once. She freely admits having an abortion herself, and has pled guilty. She has not been charged with conspiracy."

Josh looked at Becca Lloyd, the Assistant DA, as if asking for confirmation. Becca looked ahead, stifling a smile. She and Kate had been at law school together, and they had hated each other ever since.

"Hmmm." The judge scratched his nose again and examined his finger. He sniffed. "I'm inclined to believe that your client's standing in the community does not work in her favor. She's no innocent bystander in this. She wasn't raped, or assaulted. She's intelligent enough to know how to prevent a pregnancy, or to have the self-respect to abstain if she believes she is unable to do so."

Kate held herself still and quiet. She'd been dreading this since the day she'd been told that Kusak was taking their case. He was a hardline pro-lifer, always had been. In the days when abortion had been legal he'd worked to find loopholes he could use to punish women who had them and doctors who provided them. He was in his element.

"I'm sorry, Mr Zimmerman. I have no choice but to sentence your client to two months in prison, which is the maximum I am allowed under the law. Ms Mitchell, you will be taken to Carswell Medical Prison where you will spend two months in consideration of your actions and the life you chose to end. While you are there, you will repay your debt to society by providing your biological matter for use by the state in assisting those poor souls who are unable to conceive a child of their own."

She glared at Josh. *Say something.* But it was too late.

She thought back to the moments she'd spent in her car in the clinic parking lot. If she'd stayed where she was, if she'd managed to get away, would she be here? She would, she knew; they had her name on their records. And at least she'd taken the second pill before rushing back inside to help. It had worked, the baby was gone. She wouldn't be having Robert's child, thank God.

Her body froze as she thought about what she would tell Sasha.

CHAPTER THIRTEEN

THAT WOMAN WAS STARING AT CINDEE AGAIN. THE tall black woman with the big hair and the skin the color of an Americano.

Cindee didn't like it.

She found herself a seat in a corner of the dining room and shuffled her food around the tray, putting off the moment when she'd have to place it in her mouth. Cindee was used to wholesome meals, the kind of plain food that her mom said was good for the constitution. This was plain alright, to the point of being a tasteless pile of gelatinous goop. There was something that looked like it was supposed to be corn, and a slice of meat the color of a week-old dishrag. A plastic cup of tepid water and a dry cookie that tasted of sawdust.

Cindee was losing weight. Sure, her stomach was growing, but the rest of her was getting more and more bony. That doctor would give her a lecture about it next time she saw her, no doubt. The baby had to be looked after. The baby had to be fed.

She didn't want to feed it. Not now, while it was inside

her, and not later, when it wasn't. She was never going to breastfeed the thing, not ever. The thought of it made her want to puke. It made her think of him, and the things he'd done to her.

The staring woman was getting up from her chair now, clearing away her tray. Good. Maybe she'd stop staring. Cindee wondered how long she could sit in this corner before anyone else started paying attention to her. They knew she was pregnant, and they knew what she'd done. Some of them looked at her with pity, others with scorn. No one looked at her with friendship, not that she wanted any friends. Not that she deserved any.

The woman placed her tray neatly on the pile then paused to wipe her hands on the prison issue sweatpants they all wore. Cindee's were straining at the waist but hung off of her everywhere else.

Then the woman turned back toward Cindee. She looked at her and then down at the floor, in that way people have when they're watching you but they don't want you to know it.

She exchanged a few words with another black woman before waving her away and turning back to Cindee, avoiding eye contact.

The only way out of this room was through the door beyond the trash cans. Cindee was cornered. She looked from side to side, checking out the tables that flanked hers. One held a group of six women, talking and laughing like they were in a diner or something. The other had three women, eating in silence. Should Cindee move to sit with them? Would that be safer? Or would it make things worse?

It was too late. She'd spent too long thinking about it, and now the woman was in front of her. She stopped and cocked her head.

"Hey," she said.

"Hey."

"I'm Grace."

Cindee nodded.

"What's your name?"

"Cindee."

"Nice name."

Cindee shrugged.

"Mind if I take a seat?"

Cindee shook her head; she couldn't bring herself to say *go away*.

"Thanks. I just got here. Food's awful, isn't it?"

"I guess so."

"What kinda food are you used to?"

Cindee frowned. What did this woman want, her life story? "Apple pie."

"Your mom make it?"

She swallowed, thinking of her mom's apple pie. Large, juicy apples picked from their own backyard, and crisp pastry. Thick cream and sugar. "She does."

"Sounds awesome. I make blueberry pie, when there's enough blueberries. And when I have the time. Three kids means I ain't got too much of that."

Cindee shrugged; she didn't really care about this woman's baking habits.

"You got any brothers or sisters?" Grace asked.

"A sister. Suze."

"You get along OK?"

"Not too bad." The last time she'd seen Suze had been outside the clinic. She hadn't been at Cindee's trial.

"That's good. My three are at each other hammer and tongs, most of the time." The woman looked down for a moment.

"I don't mean to be rude, but I kinda like it sitting here on my own."

"You didn't look like you liked it."

Cindee snorted. "Well I'm in prison. No one likes it."

"But you like being alone."

"I do."

"Alright then. But if you ever need someone to talk to..."

"I won't."

"If you do. I'm Grace. I'm a high school teacher. You can trust me."

"Whatever."

Grace sighed and stood up. She held out her hand. Cindee stared at it for a moment then grasped the fingertips and shook them limply.

"Nice to meet you, Cindee," said Grace. "See you around." She stared walking away.

"I hope not," Cindee muttered, not quite loud enough for Grace to hear.

CHAPTER FOURTEEN

"How are you today, Grace?"

"I'm fine, thank you Doctor."

There was no point in being rude to this woman, who after all was only trying to be nice. Grace wondered how she'd got here, what had made her want to work in the prison system. It was no place for an innocent like Doctor Maya Henderson.

"Call me Maya. Please."

"Maya."

She gave Grace a smile that would have warmed her heart if it weren't aching so much. "I'm glad to hear you're doing OK. Did you manage to speak to Cindee?"

"The girl doesn't want help. She's a mess."

"I thought you'd have worked with plenty of kids like that."

"At school, I'm an authority figure. No matter how messed up they are, they know if they won't talk to me, they could get in trouble."

"Right." Maya looked down at the computer on her desk. The air-con was on high today; Grace could feel it wafting across her skin. She wished they had air-con in the cells. It was stuffy in there, even in October. Too many bodies, too much hot rage and frustration.

"I need to give you a quick exam," Maya said. She licked her lips and glanced at the camera in the corner, up by the ceiling. Grace watched her. She'd seen enough liars in her time to know there was something she wasn't being told.

"Is something wrong?"

"No. No, not at all. But it's been a week since I last checked you over. I wouldn't be doing my job if I didn't take a look at you. Check you're healing OK."

Grace nodded; she'd been feeling dull pain down below since she'd got here. She knew that whatever had happened at the hospital, it hadn't gone well.

"Fair enough." She headed for the gurney against the wall, waiting for the doctor to follow her. When she didn't, Grace grabbed the drapes herself. She started tugging at the waistband of her pants, knowing she was expected to strip from the waist down and then place the sheet of paper provided over herself. For modesty, as if there were such a thing in this place.

Maya followed her through the drapes and pulled them closed. She said nothing about Grace stripping. Instead, she gave Grace an intense look that made her feel uncomfortable.

"You need me to get undressed?" asked Grace.

Maya shook her head. Grace stared at her, puzzled.

Maya looked behind her, at the point where the drapes met the ceiling. The camera was obscured; this was one place the State of Texas was not permitted to watch.

Maya nodded a few times, looking as if she was coming to a decision. "I need to talk to you," she whispered.

Grace frowned. "What's going on?"

Maya smiled. "You don't mince your words, do you Grace?"

"In my experience working with kids, it's the best way. Don't pussyfoot round them and they pay you attention."

"I'll bear it in mind." She dropped her voice. "I want to talk to you about your results."

"You already told me. No infection, no permanent damage."

"Keep your voice down, please. Not just those results."

"You haven't done any more tests."

"No. But as you know, I was required to gather evidence."

"You said you couldn't tell me about that."

"I know."

"So?"

Maya looked up at the ceiling again. Her cheeks were flushed. Grace waited; no point rushing the woman.

Maya sat on the bed and patted it for Grace to sit next to her. Grace did so.

"It wasn't enough," Maya said.

"What d'you mean, enough?"

"I was expecting not to find any damage. Anything caused by external forces. Implements."

"You think I aborted myself with a coat hanger?"

"*I* don't. But you need to prove that you didn't. You do know they found an unraveled coat hanger in your bedroom?"

"My girl was using it to make some kind of doll for school."

"Hmm. With the results I have, I don't think there's conclusive evidence that you or anyone else used a sharp instrument. But I can't say for definite that nothing was put inside you."

"What do you mean, put inside me?"

"You were unconscious when you got to hospital. It was all very rushed. They probably used a speculum to open up your vagina. It could have scarred you. That could be what I'm seeing. Unless it's from a coat hanger, or something else."

"You think I did it."

"I do not. But I have to tell them what I see. I just wanted you to know, is all."

"So what do I do with this information?"

"Tell your lawyer."

"I don't have a lawyer."

"Everyone has a lawyer."

Grace sighed. Her stomach ached, and she wanted to sleep. "Doctor Henderson. I'm sorry to tell you this. But when you're poor and black like me, when you've got three kids at school, a husband trying to work his way out of the prison system, and a job constantly under threat from budget cuts, you don't have a lawyer."

"You have the court-appointed lawyer."

"I haven't even met him yet."

"How come?"

"My trial date hasn't been set. I guess I have to wait."

"Well, when you do meet your lawyer, tell them what I told you. Just in case the DA's office doesn't hand it over."

This was a waste of time. Grace would be allocated some spotty kid fresh out of law school, or some old guy so bored with the law he'd hardly bat an eyelid when her case came to trial. She knew how it worked. And she knew better than to believe anyone working for the State would want to help her. Even this doctor, with her sincere smile and her freshly laundered shirt.

"Just in case," she said.

"Just in case," the doctor replied.

There was a noise from beyond the curtains. They both flinched and looked toward them. Maya flicked them open; there was no one there.

"Right," said Grace. "Can I go now, or do you need to examine me?"

"You can go. Thank you."

CHAPTER FIFTEEN

THERE WAS A WOMAN ALREADY SITTING ON THE BENCH outside the chow hall. Cindee hesitated; she'd been coming out here every afternoon, and no one else had braved the chill before.

The woman turned to look at her. Her eyes were red and her mid-length dark hair disheveled. She shifted along the bench and gave Cindee a weak smile.

Afraid of being rude—she was terrified of aggravating the other inmates—Cindee perched on the opposite end of the bench, squeezed in next to the armrest. She pulled her thin jacket tighter around her shoulders.

Huddled into herself, she gazed ahead. There was a view of sorts from here, an outlook over what passed for prison grounds. A stubby patch of grass ahead of her, and the basketball court to her right. No one had used them for some weeks, she imagined. And the grass looked as if it hadn't been cut for a while.

"Hello, I'm Kate," the woman said.

Cindee tensed. She'd avoided talking to people so far, keeping to herself or hiding in crowds. Her cellmate Dora, older than her own mom, had taken her under her wing on her first night, even lent her some soap and a toothbrush. But Cindee had found it impossible to return this brusque friendliness and the woman had soon given up.

"I don't mean to be rude," the woman at the other end of the bench said. "But I've seen you around the place. You look like you could use a friend."

Cindee stared ahead, terrified. Was this a trap? Was this woman going to steal the food she'd pocketed at dinner, tell the guards she was out here when she shouldn't be? No one had stopped her coming outside so far, so she'd carried on doing it. She didn't know what she was more scared of; the women in there, with their noise and energy, or the guards who might haul her inside if they found her out here. At least out here, she could imagine the real world. Even smell it.

"Sorry. I'll leave you alone."

Cindee let herself relax a little. She didn't want to make friends here. She didn't even know how long she would be here, or if they would transfer her somewhere else when the baby was due. She wasn't all that big yet; she could disguise it with the loose prison clothes. And the rest of her was even more skinny than when they'd arrested her, a situation not helped by the prison food making her nauseous.

She was pulled out of her thoughts by movement up ahead; a van, pulling through the outside gates to the prison. Food, supplies, or newcomers maybe. She stood up, ignoring the woman at the other end of the bench, and took a few steps forward to watch. Watching even the smallest of changes to this place, observing it all, kept her sane. The way that watching her mom and dad's movements at home had kept her sane. She'd logged everything they did, each time they went out. She could predict her dad's moods more accurately than he could himself.

The van paused for the second set of gates to be opened. There was a woman at the wheel and four, maybe five people in the seats behind her. Newcomers. Cindee bit her lip, remembering her own first night.

The van stopped on the other side of the wire fence beyond the scrubby grass. Cindee glanced at the doors behind her, expecting to be steered inside at any moment. There was no one there. The woman—Kate—had followed her. She stood along from Cindee, a little farther away than she had been on the bench. Her tongue poked out between her lips.

The driver's door opened, and the guard climbed out. She was middle-aged, with short red hair and a scar on the side of her face. Cindee had seen her before, doing inspections. She had a face that made you behave yourself.

She walked round to the side door of the van, slowly, casually, like she was a mom hauling her kids out of the car for Little League. She yanked the door open and shouted something into the van. Cindee took another step forward, wondering if the new prisoners could see her in the gloom here. There was a floodlight over the van; the guard would have stopped there on purpose.

One by one, five women climbed out. Each in turn paused to take in her surroundings as her feet hit the ground. The first two women were tall and black, confident-looking. Like they knew what they were doing. The second was a petite Latina woman old enough to be Cindee's grandmother. She bent over and shuffled her feet along the ground, flinching when the guard barked at her to hurry. The fourth woman was heavy, with hair the color of ash and skin so pale Cindee felt like she might walk right through her. She looked scared.

Cindee turned back to the van to see the fifth woman climb out. She had her hand on the door and was facing away from Cindee. She had short, spiky hair dyed purple, and a tattoo that poked out from her collar.

Cindee tensed. She waited for the woman to turn, to face her. When she did, it was all Cindee could do not to cry out.

What was she doing here? Had the cops seen her at the clinic after all, when she'd taken Cindee there? Cindee had pushed her away, made sure they weren't both arrested.

Maybe she'd needed an abortion too. Maybe it was drugs.

Cindee started running. She stumbled over the uneven grass, her mind racing. She looked ahead and not down at the ground, like she should have done.

Suddenly she was flying through space. She hurtled forward, her arms thrown out. She hit the ground, her knees and elbows jarring.

She gritted her teeth, knowing better than to shout out in pain.

Kate was over her. "You OK? You went down hard."

"I'm fine." She pulled herself upright. Her hip hurt, and her arms. She felt like she'd rattled her bones out of place. She put a hand on her stomach; no movement.

"You look like you've seen a ghost."

Cindee shook her head. She turned to look towards the newcomers. She started to run again, but Kate grabbed her arm.

"You'll get into trouble. You want to spend the night in solitary?"

Cindee frowned at her, but didn't resist. Kate was right.

Kate looked past her at the new prisoners. They were filing into the building now, the guard barking at them. Cindee stared. She felt like a thousand roaches were crawling over her skin.

"You know one of them?" Kate asked.

Cindee's brain felt clogged, her body heavy. She wanted to run over there and haul her out, to demand to know why she was here. At the same time, she knew to stay put.

She swallowed. She didn't know who this Kate woman was, or if she could trust her.

"That's Suze," she said. "That's my sister."

CHAPTER SIXTEEN

Kate leaned her head on the headrest behind her, her neck muscles tensing as she moved. This bed, if it could be called that, was hard and cold, upholstered in a black PVC that she imagined would be easily wiped clean.

She smoothed down the gown she'd been told to wear, feeling the rough fabric cling to her fingertips. It was cold in here; there was a fan heater thrumming in the corner but it wasn't enough. She shivered. The bed was in the center of the room and there was nothing else here: no desk, only the one chair that the doctor sat in. No windows to see out of. Nothing to humanize the space.

The doctor put a hand on her stomach, over the gown. She flinched. She knew what to expect today; this same doctor had told her about it in her first consultation two days ago, the day after she arrived at the prison. And of course she'd been told what her sentence would involve. But that didn't make it any easier.

"You OK?" The doctor, a woman, gave her an uneasy smile.

Kate nodded. This doctor seemed like a decent woman;

she'd explained the procedure to Kate in detail, and checked she understood. She'd told her she'd be gentle. But still she was here, doing this to other women.

Kate took a deep but shaky breath. She willed her hands to be still, not to tremble from the cold. She didn't want anyone thinking she was scared; not the doctor, not the grim-faced nurse standing beyond her feet. She'd been here before, on her back, being poked and prodded. But that was when she was expecting Sasha; that had been different.

"Put your feet on the rests." The nurse had a Georgia accent, slow and relaxed. Kate lifted her head a little to find the footrests and did as she was told, feeling the rough surface bite into her bare feet.

The doctor gave her a smile and moved her hand down Kate's abdomen. "Now, lift your knees and move them to the sides, please."

Kate let her head fall back again to avoid eye contact. She stared at the ceiling. There were tiles running across it, and a light strip running down its center. The light strip was turned off; the only light now was the spotlight the doctor was using, at the bottom of the bed. Kate felt her stomach clench.

"Everything alright?" She felt as much as heard the doctor's jacket rustle as she lifted her head to look at Kate's face. Kate didn't look back, but instead nodded in silence.

She willed herself to relax, knowing this would hurt more if she tensed. But the thought of the two women staring at her, rummaging around inside her body, made it impossible.

She felt the cold speculum make contact with her skin. She winced.

"Sorry." The doctor's voice was muffled.

She felt pressure; from outside her body, where the

doctor had a hand on her stomach, and from inside, where the instruments were burrowing into her. She held her breath.

"Breathe, please."

She pushed out a thin breath and watched as the steam floated up towards the ceiling. The gown had fallen away at the back and the plastic bed was even colder now against her naked skin. She focused on the sensation, pulling her mind up and away from between her legs.

She felt a twist inside her and a tug. She gasped. Then another push and a sensation of scraping against her flesh.

She was wrong. This was nothing like when she'd had Sasha. Then, she had consented. Then, she had wanted the examinations, the fertility drugs. But now, she was being forced. Made to take a drug that would trigger ovulation and then to lie here and have her eggs removed from her body like they were the property of the state and not hers. This, more than any incarceration, was her punishment. And she would have to do it again next month.

She felt another tug. The doctor muttered something to herself. There was a sucking sensation and then the sound of a metal instrument being placed on a tray. She closed her eyes, clenching her buttocks.

The doctor draped a flimsy sheet of paper over Kate's middle. "All done," she said. She was looking at her, Kate knew. Smiling at her maybe. But Kate wasn't looking back. Instead, she pulled her gaze to the wall as she sat up on the bed and placed her feet on the floor, her legs zipped together. A dull ache had begun in her abdomen; it would get worse.

"See you in a week," said the doctor. Kate grunted.

"Come on girl, time for our next patient." The nurse

grabbed her arm and ushered her towards the door. Kate eyed her, wondering how she could be so callous.

The nurse snorted. "Can't be all that bad, can it? Not compared to what you did."

Kate felt heat rise up her neck.

She squared her jaw and pushed through the door to the corridor outside, avoiding the eye of the woman waiting after her.

CHAPTER SEVENTEEN

Brian Cho, Medical Director of the prison, paced his office. Maya sat watching him.

"You don't understand, Maya," he said.

She wasn't entirely sure what she was being accused of yet.

"This isn't your usual clinical setting," he continued. "This is a prison. These women are criminals. You can't just treat them like normal patients."

She blinked, waiting.

He stopped pacing. "I need to know you understand."

"I don't know what I'm supposed to be understanding. Have I done something, or is this just a general warning?"

He balled his fists on his hips. "Jeez Maya, you can be obtuse sometimes."

She pursed her lips, pushing down her irritation. "Tell me what I did wrong, Brian. Or what it is you need me to do different."

He sank into his chair with a sigh. The desk between them was neat, with a pad arranged in the center, its edges perpendicular to the edge of the desk. Next to it was a pot of pens. She would have bet all of them worked.

"You're getting too friendly with them. Telling them stuff they don't need to know."

"Like what?" She uncrossed and re-crossed her legs, trying not to let her anxiety show.

"Grace Williams. Manslaughter."

"She hasn't been convicted yet."

He rolled his eyes. "The case against her is pretty tight, as far as I can tell. We can expect her to be here for a while. You can't go cozying up to her."

"I gave her an internal exam. I reassured her about the healing process."

"You gave her her test results."

Her breath caught. "What makes you think that?"

"The camera, in your office?"

She frowned; she'd been careful to check the position of the camera, on the other side of the curtain. These women may not have many constitutional rights left but she knew that privacy during a medical exam was one of them.

"I don't know what you're talking about," she replied.

"We get sound, too."

"Sound?"

She ran over the conversations she'd had with patients—prisoners—over the last few weeks. She'd tried to reassure these women, to alleviate what they had to go through. What she had to put them through. She couldn't recall saying anything to the other women that would get her into trouble. But Grace. Grace was different.

He stared at her for a moment. She met his gaze, trying not to blink.

He stood up. "You're getting too close to them. It has to stop."

"I'm their doctor. They need to trust me."

He thumped the desk. "No, Maya. You work for the State of Texas. They're criminals. You don't get close to them. You don't give them their results unless I give you express permission. You don't chat to them, reassure them, butter them up. You *do your job*."

She stared at him, her heart racing.

"You understand?" he hissed. She wondered if the guard was still outside. If he could hear this.

"I understand."

"If you can't comply, I'll be forced to consider giving your job to someone else. A man, someone trustworthy."

She stood up, filled with rage. She knew better than to let it out. "I'll do as you say. My job. No more, no less."

His eyes narrowed. "You're lying."

"I don't want to lose my job." If she was fired, she might not get another job in obstetrics. Hospitals everywhere were shedding staff since Medicaid had been axed. And female staff were being let go twice as fast as the men. "I'll keep things professional."

"Good. In the meantime, I'm giving Williams to another doctor."

"You ca—"

"I can. We recruited a new gynecologist last week."

"You're replacing me."

"Don't be an idiot. We need more of you, now we have all the abortion convicts to process. Robert Abbott knows his stuff."

She felt her chest tighten. "Give her to someone else."

Brian leaned forward. "You're blushing. You know Abbot?"

"I used to." She and Robert had been at medical school

together. She knew him well, too well. "I don't think she's the right patient for him."

Brian ran a hand across his thinning hair. "This is the problem, Maya. None of them are the right patient for anyone. These goddamn women, I wish I didn't have to give them medical care. But if the state is going to take their eggs, then I have to make sure it's done properly. It's not for you to say who it is does that."

"I don't think she and Robert are well matched."

"Maya, stop it. Just stop. Now get out of my office, before I have no choice but to fire you."

CHAPTER EIGHTEEN

Kate waited outside the door to the visiting room, trying not to let the impatience get to her. At last the guard, a man with a thin mustache and arched eyebrows, let her through.

Sandra stood up, looking unsure of herself. Around them, prisoners were greeting their families, hugging and occasionally kissing, although kissing wasn't strictly allowed, to prevent the passing of objects between mouths.

Kate leaned in and gave her friend a hug. She felt Sandra push against her, relieved that Kate had taken the initiative.

Sandra pulled away and held Kate at arm's length. "How are you?" She cocked her head to one side. "Is it dreadful?"

Kate tried to laugh. "They're treating me OK," she replied, pushing thoughts of the harvesting procedure from her mind. "The food's awful, but I could lose some weight anyway."

They sat down opposite each other at the flimsy table. Sandra leaned in. "What are the other prisoners like?"

Kate frowned. Sandra was a family lawyer, not a criminal specialist like her, and got most of what she knew about criminals from the sordid novels she read.

"They're fine," Kate said. "Some of them are friendly, others you steer clear of. I'm learning which is which."

Sandra's face fell. "You'll stay safe, won't you?"

Kate laughed. "I'm locked inside three layers of security, with cameras on me day and night. It's pretty secure."

"You know what I mean. I worry about you."

"Don't. Please." Kate hated the thought that she was causing other people anxiety. She pulled on a smile. "How's the firm?

Sandra shrugged. "Tom Abad is on the warpath. His favorite client decided to go to Dean and Hewison and he's determined to find out whose fault it is."

"You mean Furman?"

"Uh-huh."

"But he doesn't let anyone else deal with them. So if they jumped, it has to be his fault....doesn't it?" Kate thought over the limited contact she'd had with Furman, an investment banker with a habit of stretching the law to breaking point. Tom, her mentor and the guy who'd hired her from law school, had always been there. Steering the meeting, making sure no one messed up. Even a senior partner like Kate wasn't immune.

"Is he mad at me?" she asked.

Sandra snorted. "You know what he thinks about the abortion law. Hates that it got passed back to being state law. If he could, he'd probably use you as a test case."

"I don't think that will work. The climate isn't what it was."

"I know." Sandra leaned in and lowered her voice. "Claude White laid off two junior partners. Both women."

White was another named partner, one Kate had never felt comfortable around. "Why?"

"One of them was pregnant. The other one asked for time off to care for her elderly mother."

"And they got fired for that?"

"They needed to cut some fat. You know it's legal now."

"Of course I do." Kate had been lucky; the American Values Amendment had been passed after Sasha started high school, and Kate could show that being a mother didn't affect her ability to work just as hard as her male colleagues. "How's Sasha?"

Sandra smiled. "She's a credit to you. She's been cooking my dinner after she gets in from school."

"Wow. How?"

A shrug. "A fridge full of food and a stove. Same way anyone cooks dinner."

"But all she knows is how to make a PBJ sandwich."

"She's been hiding her abilities from you, my friend." Sandra hesitated. "She's quite the homemaker. I caught her vacuuming last night."

Kate felt her chest tighten. Sasha would be receiving homemaking classes at school, designed to teach the girls how to care for a future husband and family. The boys had computing. All part of the drive to take America back to its so-called heyday.

"Don't let her, will you?" Kate said. "I mean, it's great that she's helping you out. But I don't want her thinking that's all she's good for."

Sandra put a hand on her friend's arm. "Don't worry. I have some shelves I'll ask her to put up. And I've been encouraging her to work her way through my divorce law books."

"Poor girl."

"I get the feeling she's doing it as a way to distract herself from something," Sandra said. "The housework, I mean."

"Oh?"

"She's preoccupied. Barely talks to me."

"I thought that was just me."

"I've tried, Kate. I know it's hard for her. You being here."

"I'll be home soon."

"Two months is a long time at fourteen."

Kate nodded. She tried to remember herself at fourteen; did time pass quickly, or relentlessly slowly? A bit of both, maybe.

"Thank you for looking after her. I appreciate it."

Sandra shrugged. "What are friends for?" She paused. "Julian's been sniffing around, though. Thinks she should be with him."

"No way. He's two thousand miles away. What about school? And that awful Monique woman."

Sandra laughed. "Yeah, she is a bitch. Don't worry. I held him off."

"Keep holding."

"I will. Sasha said something about Robert, just after you came here."

Kate's head jerked up. "He hasn't been trying to make contact with her, has he?"

"Not as far as I know. She wouldn't be happy if he did. She's made that clear."

"What did she say?"

"Just told me not to answer the phone, if he called."

Kate felt her chest hollow out. "I wish I could be there with her. I never got a chance to talk to her about him."

"What happened between you guys? One minute you

were sweetness and light, and the next he was gone. Was it the pregnancy?"

"Nothing like that." She eyed her friend. Sandra was her oldest friend, someone she'd known since law school. But this was between her and her daughter. "Just keep him away from her. He's bad news."

Sandra frowned. "Of course."

Kate grabbed Sandra's wrist. "Look after her for me, huh? Keep her safe."

"Of course I will. Don't you worry."

CHAPTER NINETEEN

"In."

Grace looked at the guard, then did as she was told. She'd been told to gather all her belongings and bring them here. She was being allocated a new cell.

"Is this permanent?" she asked.

The guard, a young woman with mousy blonde hair tied back in a severe bun, shrugged. "I was told to move you. That's all I know. Make yourself comfortable, might as well."

She clanged the door shut and left Grace alone. Grace had no idea why she'd been moved; was this something that just happened, or had she done something to deserve it? She'd been in a dorm before, sharing a cubicle with Francine who knitted constantly and muttered to herself as she did so. But at least she hadn't given Grace any trouble.

This was a proper cell, with a bunk in the corner and a cupboard next to it. A book sat on the top, next to a plastic bag containing a toothbrush and tube of toothpaste. Grace's own toothpaste, lent to her by a woman whose name she hadn't caught, had run out. She longed for more, but she hadn't been given a job here so couldn't earn the money to buy it. And no one from outside had sent her any cash.

She lifted her pile of clothes onto the top bunk, assuming that would be hers. There was another cupboard at the end of the bunk beds; she opened it and placed her underwear inside. Her t-shirts and jeans she folded neatly and slid in next to them. She didn't have much else in the way of belongings: a Bible she'd been given by another inmate and a roll of toilet paper; she'd learned on the first night she needed to keep her own stock of that.

Once everything was neatly stashed away, she considered the bed. She didn't much want to haul herself up to the top bunk, knowing that she could be called down again any moment. Dinnertime was soon, but she had no watch so didn't know just how soon. Did she dare sit on the other woman's bunk?

"Hi."

She span round to see a woman standing in the doorway. She was skinny and white, with dark, thin hair that hung around her face.

"Hello."

The woman walked in, hand extended. Grace lifted her own hand tentatively and let the woman shake it. The woman's grip was firm, her demeanor confident. Grace felt herself stiffen under the gaze of this young, self-assured white woman.

"I'm Kate."

"Grace."

"How long you got?"

"I'm on remand."

"Oh. Sorry. I've got two months. Five weeks left."

"Oh. This your bunk?" Grace gestured toward bottom bunk.

"Yeah. But you can have it, if you want."

Grace stared at her. No one gave up their bunk; she'd learned that in the short time she'd spent here. What would Kate want in return?

She shook her head. "I'll be fine up top."

"I don't mind, you know. Honest. You look like you could use being on the bottom."

Grace narrowed her eyes. "I'll be fine up top."

Kate shrugged. "If you change your mind, just tell me." She slid past Grace, careful not to make bodily contact, and perched on the bottom bunk. "I'd quite like the top bunk, really."

"So why didn't you take it when you had the chance?"

"There was someone else up there when I got here. Sharlene."

"What happened to her?"

Silence. Grace wondered if she'd asked something she shouldn't.

Kate balled her fists in her lap. "I dunno. If she finished her sentence, she didn't tell me about it."

"Maybe she didn't finish."

"Yeah." Kate looked pensive. "Maybe they moved her."

"Like they moved me."

"Like they moved you. So, you sure you don't want the bottom?"

"You don't need to patronize me, young lady."

Kate threw her hands up, palms forward. "I didn't mean to cause offense. I won't ask again."

"Hmm."

Kate lay down on the bunk, her face to the wall. Then she turned and sat up again. Grace was eyeing the top bunk, wondering how much effort it would take to get up there.

"I think you've misjudged me," Kate said.

Grace grunted. What was she supposed to say?

"You think I'm going out of my way because I'm white, and you're black. Because I'm younger than you. Because I think you look sick."

Grace felt her lip twitch. "I'm not sick."

"I saw the way you were moving, when I came in. You've got pain." She pointed to her own abdomen. "I know what they do to some of the women. I've had it too."

"I don't know what you're talking about."

Kate raised herself up on the bed. "Harvesting. I know it can hurt."

Grace's cheeks grew hot. She thought of the conversation she'd had with the doctor. This girl had no idea how lucky she was. Two months, and a simple procedure a couple of times. Then out and back to her privileged WASPy life.

"Please," Grace said. "Leave me be. I'd like to rest."

"Sorry. I'll leave you alone." Kate turned over on her bunk and fell silent. Grace watched her, wondering why she hadn't accepted the offer of that bunk.

CHAPTER TWENTY

"I need your help."

Maya eyed her patient, then looked up at the camera in the corner. "What can I do?"

"It's my cellmate. She's sick. I can tell. She's not doing so well here."

"You told me your cellmate had left."

"That was Sharlene. This is Grace."

Grace. Maya looked up at the camera again, her heart picking up pace. "Grace who?" She leaned back in her chair, watching as Kate straightened her sleeve. Maya had just given her an injection of GRH, designed to make her ovulate when they needed her to.

"Williams. Grace Williams. I've been watching the way she moves. Is she one of your patients?"

"She's with another doctor."

"Oh."

"Sorry. I'm afraid I can't help." Maya pushed the used needle into the sharps box behind her and pulled off her latex gloves. She opened the trash can and dropped them inside.

Kate stood up. She rubbed her arm where the needle had gone in. The needles they used for this hormone were thick and long. Plenty of women had resisted the injection, prompting Maya to call a guard to help her administer it. She'd been relieved when Kate hadn't caused trouble.

"What's her doctor like? Is she like you?" Kate asked.

Maya let out a breath. "I can't talk to you about the other staff, I'm afraid. I'm sure you understand."

"Are you OK?"

"Me?"

"You seem… different."

Maya glanced at the camera again, wishing she could stop herself from doing that. She wondered if Brian was listening. "I'm fine. Just doing my job." She blushed, aware that she might sound as if she was mocking her boss. "You can take that Band-Aid off in a half hour or so."

Kate patted her sleeve. "Thanks. If you could talk to your colleague, maybe. About Grace. I'm worried about her."

"I'm sure if she has any medical problems then my colleague will be able to identify those for himself."

"Himself? A man?"

"Half of the medical staff here are men. More."

"OK. But if you can say something to him, about Grace. She's been slowing down. I think she's in pain. And she cries, at night."

"Plenty of women here cry at night."

"That doesn't make it alright though, does it?"

Maya looked at this woman, who she'd persuaded to trust her. *I'm here to make it easier on you*, she'd said to her, to all of them. She'd given them false hope, made them think there was someone here who cared about them.

She'd lied.

"I'm sorry, Kate. This isn't appropriate. I suggest you focus on yourself. You need to get through the next five weeks and get out of here. It isn't long now."

"Feels like a lifetime."

"It'll be gone in no time, I promise."

"Who'll watch over Grace, when I'm gone?"

"I'm sure her next cellmate will. And her doctor." She felt herself tense at the thought of Robert, the kind of care he gave these women. "You shouldn't worry. It's not your concern."

Kate shrugged. "OK. Thanks, Doctor."

"May..." Maya began, but then thought better of it. Kate closed the door behind her, her footsteps slapping along the corridor. No one came in to take her place. Was it time to go home, already?

Maya sighed, thinking of her empty apartment. Kate had a daughter waiting for her outside, and maybe a husband or boyfriend. Her life would return to normal quicker than she knew.

Maya sat in silence, listening to her breathing, drawing up the energy to pack away her things. She patted her cellphone in her pocket, expecting a call from Brian at any moment. But it stayed quiet.

She flinched when a knock came at the door.

"It's open." She plastered on a smile, waiting for another dressing down. But it was her next patient; she'd got the time wrong.

"Come in," she breathed, more relieved than she expected.

CHAPTER TWENTY-ONE

CINDEE COULD FEEL THE LETTER SITTING INSIDE HER bra like it was going to burn a hole in her skin. All the way through breakfast, while she was working in the laundry, and during lunch. She felt her fingers flutter to it again and again, desperate to retrieve it, to open it. But she knew better.

At last it was afternoon and she had some free time. Her cell mate was out working in the kitchens and the dorm was quiet. She shuffled onto her bunk, listening to the bed springs creak under her weight. She was getting fatter: almost six months pregnant now and her belly was gross despite her starvation diet. She hated it.

She looked toward the door, listing intently. She could hear a woman in the showers at the end of the hall, singing to herself as she soaped down. The showers got busy at the beginning and the end of the day; some women would brave the cold water to use them in the afternoons, when there was some privacy.

She turned toward the wall, curled around her own hideous belly. She pushed a hand inside her bra, which strained to contain her swelling breasts, and pulled the paper out.

It was folded in four, an ordinary sheet of paper. The kind of note her mom used to make shopping lists. She turned it over in her hand, savoring it. Half anticipating and half dreading the contents.

Slowly she teased it open, as quietly as she could, until it lay flat on the mattress. She huddled over it to read, the writing scratchy where the pen had given out in places.

Cindee,

I got your message from a woman called Reena. She said her friend Mona was in your block. I hope I can trust them to get this back to you.

Don't worry about me, Cin. Look after yourself. I'm a dumb idiot who let you-know-who get the better of me, and I paid the price. I spent my whole life pretending to be brave, like I was some kind of hero, and it was all chicken shit. I'm a fraud, Cin. He was doing it to me too all that time, and I didn't have the guts to tell you. Both of us at the same time. I'm so sorry.

I'm not the sister you thought I was. I'm weak, and useless, and a liar. Keep away from me. Look after yourself. You can get out of here after you have your baby and you can get a place of your own. Focus on that, girl. Your future.

I got fifteen months in here. I helped other girls get abortions too, and they found out about that. The other girls got caught because I wasn't careful enough. I didn't tell you how I knew about the clinic, Cin. I'm sorry.

Don't write me again. I'm not worth it.

Your sister,

Suze.

Cindee read the letter twice, then twice more. She folded it up again, put it back inside her bra, then got it out and read it once more. She leaned back and stared at the wall. She felt empty, like the life had been sucked out of her.

Suze had given up. So she'd lied; that didn't matter. It was his fault. It was all his fault.

But one thing was for sure: Cindee wasn't going to get herself a place and build herself and this baby a cozy little life when she got out of here. She owed her sister more than that. She wouldn't ignore her; she would help her. Suze had always been the strong one; now it was Cindee's turn.

Just exactly how she would do that, she had no idea.

CHAPTER TWENTY-TWO

MAYA SLID ALONG THE HALLS, AWARE THAT SHE LOOKED out of place. Some of the medical staff liked to stray outside the clinical suite and keep an eye on the women in their cells; she didn't. It was permitted, if not encouraged; they were doctors and had the right to go wherever they wanted. But she didn't like to be reminded that the women she treated were locked up at night.

She arrived at Grace's cell. She'd taken the trouble to check Grace's cellmate would be out. Kate Mitchell, who she'd had for harvesting a couple of weeks ago. Kate's was a clear case; she'd been caught by the cops at an abortion clinic, a pill packet in her car and her name on the appointment book. She'd pled guilty, and been sentenced to 'donate' her eggs. Maya didn't like being the one to take them, but guessed if someone had to do it, it was better her than one of the other doctors. Especially Robert Abbott.

She'd also checked Grace's work schedule. Grace would be in her cell.

She arrived at Grace's cell. The door was open. She knocked and put her head round the door.

"Doctor? Everything alright?"

She smiled. "Everything's fine, don't worry. I just wanted a chat. Can I come in?"

Grace shrugged. "Not much I can do to stop you."

Maya pushed aside the cold reception. She stepped inside the room and hesitated. Should she sit on the bed, or remain standing?

Standing was best.

"I have something you need to know about," she said.

Grace had been washing her hands at the sink. She wiped them dry on a t-shirt that was hanging over a chair and sniffed. "Like what?"

Maya leaned in, lowering her voice. "Your blood test."

Grace stiffened. "Uh huh."

"Grace, did you drink raspberry leaf tea when you were pregnant?"

Grace turned to her. "Did I *what*?"

"Raspberry leaf tea. It brings on contractions. Did you take it?"

"I drank herbal teas. Didn't want caffeine doing any damage to the baby. I can't remember which I had."

"Did no one warn you of the risks?"

A shrug. "It was just fruit tea. Are you telling me I drank something that killed my baby?" Grace had paled.

Maya put a hand on her shoulder. Grace tensed but didn't push it off. Contact was disallowed between inmates, but not between doctor and patient.

"I'm so sorry, Grace. I think it might have brought on the miscarriage."

"That's rubbish, and you know it. The baby was sick. It wasn't *viable*. I did nothing wrong."

Maya reached a hand out but Grace pulled away. "I

know you didn't mean to. But juries don't tend to look favorably on this kind of thing. Not anymore."

"It's just herbal tea! How was I to know?"

"They'll say you should have read the label."

Grace slumped. "I have to get out of here. I have to get back to my babies." She looked up. "Sissy and the boys."

Maya's throat felt sore. "I know." She leaned in. "And I can help you with that."

"How?" Maya's voice was thick.

"The less I tell you, the less you'll be able to tell them."

A nod.

"Just trust me, OK?"

"Why? Why should I trust anyone?"

Maya looked at Grace, feeling helpless. This was ridiculous. This woman had made a stupid mistake, and now she was going to be made to pay for it with her freedom and the future of her family.

"Just trust me, OK?"

"Guess I got no choice."

CHAPTER TWENTY-THREE

"Lawyer visit."

Kate was folding sheets. The laundry was steamy today, despite the November cold outdoors, and her shirt was drenched in sweat.

She looked at Pam, the inmate in charge of her laundry team. Pam gave her a nod of acknowledgement but looked irritated. One woman being taken away to see her lawyer meant more work for the rest of them.

"Can I change first?"

"No time." It was the same guard she'd met on her first night, an overweight woman with short black hair and a square jaw.

"I'm dripping with sweat. It'll take me a second to put on clean clothes."

"Did you not hear me the first time? Your lawyer is waiting for you. Move."

She looked back at the laundry team, who were all ignoring her. Maybe she should stop resisting authority, stop expecting people to be reasonable. But she was a lawyer; she was used to the professionalism of the courtroom, where even the judge treated you with respect if you earned it.

She smoothed down her growing hair, pushing strands back into the elastic band she'd used to tie it back, then tugged at her shirt sleeves. She unrolled them and buttoned them at the wrist. She smelled of sweat and laundry powder. Josh would have to put up with it.

She followed the guard along the corridors to the visiting rooms. There were special rooms for meeting lawyers, glass-walled but enclosed. The guards could watch you, but they couldn't listen in. Unless they had the rooms bugged, which wouldn't surprise her.

At last they reached the visiting rooms. The sweat was drying on her skin and she felt chilly away from the machines in the laundry room. She shivered.

The guard hurried her into one of the meeting rooms, not stopping to speak. She pulled the door behind her and stood in the corridor.

Kate looked at the man sitting on the chair opposite her. He was short and slim with blond hair that curled into the back of his collar. His suit looked cheap.

"Where's Josh?"

The man stood up and stretched his hand towards her. Confused, she took it and gave it a shake. He motioned toward the chair on her side of the table, but she didn't sit.

"I'm sorry, I think they brought me to the wrong room," she said. She turned back to the door, ready to knock on it.

"Kate Mitchell?" The man asked. She turned to him.

"Yes. Do you work with White, Petersik and Abad? I don't recognize you."

He coughed. "I'm a fourth-year associate."

"How come I've never met you? Where's Josh? He's working on my parole."

"That's my job now. I'm your lawyer."

"I'm sorry." She tried to keep the anger out of her voice. "But you aren't. There's been a mix up. I appreciate you coming here, but I'm wasting your time." She trained back to the door.

"Please," he said. "Just sit down, and I'll explain."

Explain what? She eased herself into the chair, watching him. If he was a new associate, he was a little old. She knew everyone else.

He gave her a nervous smile. "Your case has been handed over to me."

"You said that. You're new, I guess? Where were you before?"

"Wright and Chase."

She nodded. "OK. What's your name?"

"Lawrence Young."

"Look, I don't mean any offense Lawrence, but I'm a senior partner. Josh Zimmerman is my lawyer. He's a junior partner. I'm expecting him."

"He's busy on another case."

"What case? Josh is perfectly capable of handling more than one case at a time, you know."

Lawrence shrugged. "Sorry. That's just what I've been told. I've been working with Josh a while, I know about your case. I've done my research."

She sighed. All they needed to do was get her through her parole hearing. She didn't really need a junior partner for that; she didn't attend parole hearings in her own cases, after all.

But then, her cases weren't defending senior partners in the firm.

She sighed. "Go on then. Tell me the plan."

"I can guide you through the parole process." He hesitated. "That is, unless you already…"

"It won't do me any harm to be reminded." It was years since she'd helped a client with a parole hearing; most of them didn't get that far.

He looked relieved. "Great. I mean—"

She threw him a smile. "I know what you mean."

"OK. So I'll guide you through the parole process, prepare you. And then, assuming you pass, you'll be released."

"That simple," she said.

"Er, yeah."

She eyed him. He tugged at the collar of his shirt. "Do you know what they do women in here, Lawrence?"

The associate looked confused. "Er, yes."

"They take our eggs. They treat us like meat."

"I'm sorry. It must be tough."

She waved a hand. "I'm only here two months. There are other women here much worse off than me."

"I suggest you focus on your own case."

"You're right I guess." She pulled up her chest. "Do you have any news about my daughter?"

"Your daughter?" He fumbled through the file on the desk between them. "I didn't know about a…"

She sighed: *associates*. "Don't worry. Sandra's looking after her. I'll see her soon."

"You will."

"Good." She pushed down the guilt. "Now, talk to me about my parole hearing."

CHAPTER TWENTY-FOUR

Maya was packing her things away for the evening when there was a knock on her office door. She looked at her watch, then checked her screen. She had no more appointments today.

"Come in."

The door opened.

"Brian," she said. "Not often we see you along here."

"Not often I discover something like I found out today."

She felt her skin prickle. "Anything I can help with?"

He closed the door. "It is."

She waved him to the chair normally reserved for patients, trying to stay calm. Brian Cho never came to the gynecological consulting rooms; he found what Maya practiced vaguely distasteful, preferring his own, cleaner discipline of psychiatry.

She put her bag on the floor, hoping she wouldn't be too late home to enjoy the takeout she'd promised herself.

"What can I help you with, Brian?"

"I found evidence that you've been tampering with patient results."

She stared at him. "I've what?"

"You heard me. Do you have anything to say?"

She held her head steady. "Can you tell me exactly what results I'm accused of *tampering with*?'

He stood up and moved to the opposite wall, perusing the framed certificates and the picture she'd bought from Target.

He cleared his throat. She stared at him, her breathing short.

"Brian? What are you talking about?"

He turned to her. "So you aren't going to come clean."

"I don't know what it is I need to come clean about."

"Don't make it worse for yourself, Maya."

"Please. Just tell me what I'm being accused of."

"I had an email from Travis County Hospital. A duplicate of one they sent us a month back. Seems their systems went on the fritz and started processing requests that had already been done."

"OK." She waited for him to elaborate.

"Maya, you know what I'm referring to here. I'm giving you the chance to confess what you did. Maybe I can put a word in for you with the Board, if you can at least do that."

"At least tell me which patient it relates to. Maybe that will jog my memory."

"You know which *inmate* it refers to. We've already spoken about her."

"We speak about a lot of the women."

He sighed. "Very well, if you're going to be like that. It's Grace Willams."

She held his gaze. "Grace."

"The email held her test results from when she was admitted to the ER. Physical exam, bloodwork. That kind of thing."

She felt her body temperature drop.

"You'd sent me your report on her just yesterday," he said. "It was still on my desk"

She swallowed.

"Maya, are you going to explain to me why her test results from the ER are different from the ones we have on file here? Why the attachment to that email doesn't reflect her online records?"

She leaned forward. "How should I know? You sure the email has the right attachment?"

"It's a scan. Of a printout. Seems the attending was old-school."

Old-school, she thought. A dinosaur, more like. She'd printed off that attachment. She'd deleted the email. She'd taken the document home and put it down the waste disposal.

"How do you know it's the right document? The attachment."

Brian took a step forward. "Maya, don't."

"Don't what? I'm trying to get to the bottom of this, same as you are."

"Don't lie to me, Maya. If you told me the truth, I could defend you. You're a damn good doctor. I don't want to have to suspend you."

"Suspend me?"

"If this is what I think it is, you could be struck off."

She met his gaze. "It's not what you think it is."

"Well, you have to prove that to me. You have a fortnight."

"Brian, don't be—"

"I'm suspending you with immediate effect. There'll be a hearing, in two weeks. I suggest you go home and get your story straight."

CHAPTER TWENTY-FIVE

Cindee had always found the chow hall scary. All those women, crowded in together. Sure, a few of them had been friendly. Dora, her cellmate, had given her some soap and toothpaste on her first night. And Kate, the skinny woman she'd encountered the night Suze had arrived; she'd tried to make friends, sitting next to Cindee at breakfast the next morning. Cindee hadn't been in the mood for talking. Keep herself apart, and maybe people would leave her alone.

Today was no different. Cindee had shuffled through the line, muttering her thanks to the large woman who'd dolloped oatmeal onto her tray. Cindee didn't want to be friendly, but she sure wasn't going to be rude.

Now she was huddled over a table in the far corner, greasy hair framing her tray like a curtain. The cutlery was plastic and flimsy. Her spoon would barely contain a mouthful of the thick gloop that passed for oatmeal, and she had nothing to spread the sickly-sweet jelly on her toast.

She thought of the oatmeal her mom would make on the occasions cold weather came to her hometown. Rich and creamy, flavored with blueberries and a squeeze of maple syrup. Her dad would always get the first bowlful. She and Suze would sit in silence, their eyes on the table while he worked through his breakfast. He liked to finish before anybody else ate; that way, if he wanted extra helpings, there was no chance somebody else would have eaten it all. Not that Cindee had any appetite when he was in the room.

Once he'd had his fill, Mom would reheat the oatmeal and Cindee and Suze would get their share, able to breathe again once Dad had left the table. It wasn't that he was mean to them; quite the opposite. He was friendly and attentive. Too friendly and attentive. It made the skin on Cindee's back crawl like there was a ton of cockroaches swarming all over her.

Looking back, how had she not spotted that he was doing it to Suze too?

She lifted the oatmeal to her mouth and closed her eyes. Resisting the urge to gag, she swallowed. It was lumpy and viscous, gray like her gym shoes before Mom bleached them.

She managed to eat the full bowl. Her counselor had told her that if she didn't eat, she would be put on a special diet. Next to the oatmeal was a single slice of limp white toast. She didn't need to eat that too, surely.

She looked up, preparing for her exit. She preferred to wait for the right moment; just enough women that she wouldn't stand out, but not so many that she'd have to fight her way through.

There were four other women at the table she'd chosen, all of them young and all skinny and white, like her. Two of them had terrible teeth, brown-stained with gaps at the front. She ran her tongue over her own orthodontist-perfect teeth. They felt furry; the tooth-brushes here were flimsy and ineffective, not like her electric brush at home.

The room was busy, women pushing past each other to find a seat, voices rising in the echoing space. Two COs stood to one side, one by each door. They were both silent, their eyes roaming the room.

Then she saw her. Her roots were growing out, but Suze's purple crop was unmistakable. Cindee felt her back straighten and her breathing slow.

Suze was heading for the serving hatch, chatting with two other women like this was just the school canteen. Suze had led a tight-knit gang of misfits who scoffed at the more popular kids. They wore their weirdness like a badge of honor, reveling in the stares and murmurs that followed them as they prowled the halls. They were smart, too: smart enough to push the rules so far, but not far enough to get themselves expelled. Some of the staff hated them, while others gave them a grudging respect.

Cindee watched Suze shuffle along the line, pausing for a brief conversation with the heavy-set woman serving the oatmeal. At last she reached the end of the line. Cindee held herself upright, poised. Waiting.

Suze turned to face the room. The dark-skinned girl next to her said something and she laughed. She raised her head to scan the room.

Under Suze's left eye, which had previously been hidden, was a bruise. It was heart-shaped, centered just above Suze's cheekbone. And it was only just beginning to turn yellow at the edges, which meant it was fresh.

Cindee stepped forward, leaving her tray on the table. She heard muttering behind her but ignored it.

"Hey, bitch!" someone called. Cindee felt tension ripple

through her—in the outside world those words would reduce her to tears—but she blinked the words away.

She made her way through the space, feeling bodies brush against hers, ignoring the insults. Someone jostled her and she muttered an apology. She picked up speed.

At last she was standing in front of her sister. Suze's expression was dark, just like the time Cindee had gone to the 7-11 for some milk and caught Suze smoking behind a dumpster. Cindee had been twelve, Suze fifteen.

"Cin."

"Suze." She lifted her fingers but Suze shrank back. The woman next to her sucked her teeth. No touching in prison: a rule strictly enforced. Even between sisters.

"What happened?" Cindee asked. She lowered her voice. "Your cheek."

Suze frowned. Her fingers fluttered at her side, as if she was resisting an urge to touch the bruise.

"Did you get it?"

Now it was Cindee's turn to frown. "Yes, I got it. But I didn't know..."

"This bitch bothering you, Suze?" The tall woman who had made Suze laugh took a step forward.

"No," said Suze. "It's fine." No introductions.

"Who did this?" Cindee looked between the group of women. It wouldn't be them. Suze was too smart to hang with the kind of girls who would hurt her.

Or at least, she had been.

"I told you, Cin. Look out for yourself. You don't need me cluttering up your life."

Suze had helped her when she'd tried to self-abort. She'd taken her to the clinic, she'd made the appointment. She would have been arrested too, if Cindee hadn't pushed her out of the way when they were being chased.

If Suze wasn't helping Cindee now, when they were both in prison, then it meant something was seriously wrong.

"Can I help?" Cindee asked. "Do you need me?"

Suze gave her a sad smile, a smile that spoke of their shared history. Suze was the tough one, Cindee the good one. Suze had never needed Cindee's help in her life.

"Leave it." Suze's voice was hard. "Just look after yourself. Forget about me."

"Don't be absurd." Cindee leaned in. "Did one of the other prisoners do this to you?"

Suze's eyes were cold. "No."

"Who, then?"

Suze glanced toward the door. One of the COs was advancing on them.

"No one."

"No one?"

"No one you'll have met. Just leave it, huh?"

The tall woman muttered in Suze's ear and they both took a step back. The CO was behind Cindee.

"Everything OK, ladies? You're holding up the line." It was Smith, the sarcastic guard who'd strip-searched Cindee when she arrived.

Suze plastered on a smile. "All fine, Cindee's just leaving." She narrowed her eyes at her sister.

Cindee's legs felt hollow. The oatmeal was churning in her stomach, making her nauseous.

"Very well. Cindee, get back to your cell."

Cindee sniffed and gave Suze one last look. Suze turned away, her expression sadder than Cindee had ever seen it.

CHAPTER TWENTY-SIX

Maya didn't know how much longer she could bear staring at the walls of her apartment.

She'd tried reading a book but didn't have the focus. When switching from a medical journal to a novel she'd been meaning to read for two years hadn't worked, she'd tried turning on the TV. She'd flicked through the channels, depressed by the news and bored by the mix of home makeover shows and reality TV.

She'd even tried cooking, pulling out her grandmother's recipe for chilaquiles and filling a few nervous, ill-at-ease hours with stirring and chopping. She'd eaten the chilaquiles slowly, surprising herself with how spicy she'd made the sauce and staring out of the window, her gaze unfocused.

She sat on a chair in the window now, watching the two boys from the apartment below hers playing in the street. She remembered them as little kids, barely old enough for kindergarten. But somehow the years had passed and they were growing up, the older one rolling his eyes at his little brother every time he missed the baseball hoop.

RACHEL MCLEAN

She heard rustling outside the door to her apartment and turned, startled. Nobody knew she was here; she hadn't told what few family and friends she had that she'd been suspended. Her ex, who'd shared this place with her until eighteen months earlier, was living on the west coast now and would no more care about her job worries than he did when they'd been together.

The rustling behind the door stopped and an envelope slid through the mail slot. The girl downstairs, big sister of those boys, liked to distribute mail around the apartment block. Maya sometimes gave her a dollar for her trouble. She shuffled toward the door, listening for the sound of the girl retreating. She picked it up from the mat. It was a formal letter, the address typewritten.

She thumbed it open, hoping it was just a bill. It wasn't. Instead, it was a summons to her formal disciplinary hearing three days from now. It would be held at the prison. She wondered who would be there. Her boss, of course, but who else? She'd been a member of a union until just over a year ago, but then they had banned union membership, claiming it meant divided loyalties. If she wanted representation, the letter said, she could bring a colleague.

She wasn't about to do that. Despite being employed by the prison service, she'd never felt a true part of the team, being a medic rather than a corrections officer. Her only regular colleague in B wing was Paula, the nurse who dished out meds to the addicts and psychiatric cases every morning. Now Paula would be doing her rounds with Robert Abbott. Maya had known him in med school; she'd dated him, briefly. Both things she preferred to forget.

A shiver ran down her back at the thought of Robert having unfettered access to all those women, and as much power over them as he chose to exercise. Robert was a man

112

with a hazy sense of what constituted consent, something she'd discovered on their second date when he'd taken her *no* for a *yes*. If she hadn't had a can of Mace on her...

She folded the letter and placed it in a kitchen drawer. She needed air.

Sliding a denim jacket over her khakis and t-shirt, she slipped down the stairs, careful to be quiet. If Mrs Rees downstairs heard her moving about at this time of day, she would come out to chat. Maya didn't have the energy for conversation.

Outside, dusk was creeping up on the town. She paused to sniff the cooling air. She could smell frying bacon from the diner on the corner, despite it being long since breakfast.

She'd come out here with no real purpose, no mission. She didn't even have her purse, just a few bills in her back pocket. She could do a little grocery shopping.

She crept along the streets, anxious not to draw attention to herself. At Wholefoods she pushed inside. The store was brightly lit and welcoming in the descending evening.

She grabbed some apples, a loaf of wheat bread and a quart of milk. She had just enough in her pocket. The assistant gave her a suspicious look as she fumbled through her cash and handed it over. Or was she imagining it? She tapped her foot, eager to be home, as the man placed items in a large paper sack and handed them over with a blank smile.

Outside, she felt her breathing loosen. Darkness had fallen while she was in the store, and the temperature had dropped. She pulled her jacket tighter and hugged the bag to her chest.

Up ahead, a woman stood at a bus stop. She wore a green dress that shimmered in the streetlight, and over it a blue leather jacket. She was only a little younger than Maya but her bright clothes made her look glamorous and full of life.

Maya slowed as she approached. There was something familiar about this woman, but Maya couldn't place her. Before taking the job at the jail, she'd worked at the town's only STD clinic. It made bumping into potential former clients an uncomfortable experience. She lowered her gaze as she prepared to pass, her heart picking up speed.

Two figures were approaching from the opposite direction, ambling along the sidewalk as if they had not a care in the world. Two young guys, full of confidence and swagger.

The woman at the bus stop looked round. She tensed as she saw the men, then looked back at Maya, her eyes bright.

Maya blinked at her, wishing she could bring herself to smile.

"Hey, gorgeous," one of the men said. His voice was low and languorous, pure Texan.

The woman tensed, her eyes still on Maya. Maya stopped walking, holding the woman's gaze.

"Ya not talking to me?" the man asked.

The woman shifted from one foot to another. Maya hesitated, considering backing off and retreating the way she had come. But the fear in the woman's eyes held her rooted to the spot.

The man was right behind the woman. His friend stood behind him, sniggering. They both wore gray hoodies: one Gap, the other with a fraternity logo. They couldn't have been more than twenty years old.

"Hey, bitch," said the man whose hand was on the woman's shoulder. "Cat got your tongue?" Maya took a step toward them.

"Please," the woman said. "I'm just waiting for my bus. I don't want no trouble." She was still staring at Maya.

The man's fingers crept toward the woman's neck. She closed her eyes then opened them again.

"I'm just being friendly," the man said, his voice like sour treacle. "Don't cost nothin'."

The woman said nothing.

There was a flash of movement and suddenly the woman was twisted away from Maya, facing the man. He grinned at her, his hands firm on her shoulders and his teeth white in the glow from the streetlamp.

"Don't know what ya got to be so fussy about, " he said. "You're not even pretty."

The woman relaxed a little. Maya held her breath. The other man, pale-skinned with acne peppering his chin, looked at her over his companion's shoulder.

"You'll do, though," the first man said. The woman gasped as he pulled her to him and grabbed her collar. Maya heard fabric tearing.

"Leave her alone." Maya cleared her throat. "Leave her alone," she repeated, more clearly this time.

The man's gaze slid to Maya. He raised an eyebrow.

"What's it to do with you?" he snapped.

"Leave her be," Maya replied. Her body felt light and her head was starting to spin.

The man barked out a laugh. He plunged his hand inside the collar of the woman's dress. She whimpered.

The man turned to his acne-ridden friend. "We got one each, Dave."

Dave blushed, his cheeks blotchy. "Uh, yeah."

The first man grabbed the woman's buttocks with the hand that wasn't inside her dress. "Nice," he said. "Firm." He pulled her to him and started yanking down her dress. He grabbed the gauzy fabric and tugged. The woman cried out.

"Uh, Doug," his companion said. "Maybe we should..."

Doug had his hand on the woman's face, pulling it toward his own. "Shut up, Dave. Just fuckin' get to it."

Maya swallowed the bile that had been accumulating in her mouth.

"I'm calling the cops." She plunged her hand into her back pocket.

Her phone wasn't there.

She'd left it on the table at home, along with her purse. All she had was her keys and almost two dollars in change. And the sack of groceries.

"You're doing no such thing, bitch." The first man, Doug, took his hands off the woman. He pushed her to one side. She looked back at Maya, her eyes bright. She shook her head and then ran away. The second man threw out a hand to stop her but she was too quick.

The woman's footsteps echoed in the deserted street. Maya wondered when the bus would arrive, and how the woman would get home with it.

She turned away from the men. She would find another route home. Failing that, she would go back to Wholefoods. They would let her use the phone. She hoped.

"Stop!"

She dropped her groceries and started to run. She could hear footsteps behind her, two pairs. Over them was the sound of her own breathing.

A hand grabbed her arm, stopping her in her tracks. She stumbled but managed to stay upright.

She tugged as hard as she could, and freed herself. Struggling to regain her balance, she started to run again.

She'd taken a wrong turn. Up ahead wasn't the grocery store, but a high fence surrounding a parking lot. She felt panic grip her limbs but found the strength to turn into a side street.

"Dave! That way!"

She felt movement behind her. The air stirred. She put up a hand, waving it blindly. Up ahead was a solitary street-lamp, fizzing and blinking.

She focused on it and dragged herself forward. She wondered what had happened to the woman, hoped she'd called the cops.

She felt something hard slam into her back, winding her. She paused for a split second then carried on running.

Again it hit her, a hard cylindrical object. He caught her across the back of the knees this time. She stumbled and threw her arms out. Her palms hit the ground, closely followed by the rest of her.

"I told you to mind your own business, bitch."

She pushed up to her hands and knees. Her palms were bleeding, and her knees felt like they'd been sliced by a blade. She turned to face him.

He was standing over her, a dark cylindrical object raised above him. His friend stood next to him, staring at her.

She looked at the second man. "Help me."

His eyes widened.

"Shoulda thought of that before you decided to inter-vene," said his friend. He was panting, adrenaline coursing through his body as much as it was through hers.

There was a swift movement: the pipe, coming down at her. She lifted her hand to protect herself, too late.

CHAPTER TWENTY-SEVEN

Few of the women went outdoors in the dark before dawn, despite having the freedom to move around so they could get to work early. Kate welcomed any opportunity to be outdoors, no matter that a fine mist of drizzle bathed her skin; her clothes were damp within a minute. Her legs shook with cold, so hard it felt like they might fall off.

She sat on the bench furthest from the floodlights, her body angled against their glare. She pulled the collar of her t-shirt up, wishing she'd worn a hoody. The lights cast sharp shadows on the path in front of her: her own body, silhouetted hazily on the ground.

She wrapped her arms around herself and rubbed, trying to inject some warmth back into her cold skin. She breathed in, trying to imagine she was outside in her own backyard at home, watching the sun rise.

Two women stood across from her, under an overhanging roof. They were smoking. The jail was introducing a smoking ban in two weeks and they were encouraging the woman to smoke their supplies beforehand. It meant a constant stink of secondhand smoke throughout the building, clinging to people's clothes and hair. It reminded Kate of the summer she'd quit, in her third year of law school. It would be so easy to travel back in time, to give in to the craving. She kept as far away from the smokers as she could, turning her back when someone tried to trade one with her. Hell, there were so many to be smoked by the deadline that women were practically giving them away.

The door to the prison clanged open, dim light spilling out. Two women emerged, both fumbling with cigarette packets, not speaking to each other. One of them was Grace.

Kate watched Grace, unease growing. Kate's parole hearing had gone well; she would be leaving today. She felt a need to make amends.

She stood slowly, shaking out her prison-issue sweats. Two more women had come outside, talking between themselves.

Day was breaking and the prison was coming to life. Kate liked to wake early and come out here in the calm of the morning, before assaulting her stomach with the slop they called breakfast. Her stomach was rumbling now, but she wouldn't eat. Too nervous about her release.

Grace huddled against a wall, hugging herself for warmth. Kate wondered why she'd come out here; did she smoke, or was she meeting someone? Maybe she liked the connection to the sky, like Kate did.

Kate stopped ten paces away from Grace. "Hey," she said, injecting a confidence she didn't feel into her voice.

Grace looked up. When she recognized Kate, her face fell. "Hey."

"I'm sorry about what happened between us," Kate said. Grace shrugged.

"I just wanted to clear the air."

Grace frowned. "'Course. It's your last day."

"I have this irrational fear that they'll forget about me, and I'll just be left in my bunk, waiting."

"You'll be fine."

"Look, I meant what I said. If you need any help, legal or otherwise. I can contact your family, once I'm out."

"No point in that."

"Oh?"

"My husband's in prison too."

"Oh."

Grace snorted. "Yeah, not so keen on helping me now, are you? A woman from a family of criminals."

Kate felt heat rise up her neck. "I didn't say that."

"You thought it, though. Why don't I just save you some trouble, huh? I won't ask for your help and you don't need to offer it. You can just leave here and get on with your comfortable life."

Kate had nothing to say to that. She knew she was more fortunate than the majority of the women here. She had a friend who was coming to collect her, a nice home to go back to, and a job that was being held open for her. She knew what it meant to tick the 'ex-con' box on job applications; she'd rejected enough of those herself.

"I mean it," she said. "I'm a lawyer. If you need my help..."

"Gonna give me your card, are you? I couldn't afford it anyway. I see your shiny hair, and your clear skin. Even in here, you look expensive."

"I wouldn't expect you to pay me."

Another snort. "I don't need no charity."

Kate looked at her, wondering if she should mention

what she had heard in the nights. Grace was troubled. She was sick.

"Mitchell!"

Kate turned to see a CO standing at the open doorway, hands on hips. She felt her heart lift.

The CO tapped her foot. "Get your stuff together. Time to ship out."

Kate nodded her head. She looked at Grace. "Good luck."

Grace made a guttural sound. If she didn't want Kate's help, then who was Kate to force it on her? She was going home. She was going to see Sasha.

"Mitchell. I don't have all day."

"Sorry." She scuttled past the CO, toward her cell. She'd already gone through all her stuff last night, giving what she didn't need to other women and placing the rest of it on her bunk.

She grabbed the meager pile of belongings: a photo of Sasha, a book Sandra had brought in for her, some letters from her father in Wisconsin. She'd heard nothing from her mom, despite writing her before her trial. Her mom lived in a trailer park in Arizona; she had no interest in her daughter unless it was for money. She hadn't even seen Sasha since her granddaughter was eight years old.

An hour or so later, she was outside. The gate clanged shut behind her and she stood on the edge of the parking lot, gulping in deep breaths. She could still make out the metallic tang of the prison. It was mixed with other smells, smells she'd almost forgotten. Car exhausts, a trash can somewhere. The faint smell of stagnant water.

A car pulled up. Inside, a small woman waved at her, her face animated. Kate felt relief flood through her.

Sandra jumped out, grabbed Kate's plastic bag of

belongings and dumped it in the trunk. She hurried to the passenger door and opened it with a flourish.

"Your carriage awaits."

Kate gave her a weak smile. The adrenaline of release had washed away and she was exhausted.

"Thanks." She slid into the seat and Sandra closed the door. She darted round the front of the car, slapping the hood with the flat of her hand.

Sandra was breathless as she dove into her own side of the car. She leaned over to give Kate a hug. Kate collapsed into it, forcing down tears.

"Where's Sasha?"

Sandra stiffened in her arms.

"What day is it?" Kate had lost track. "Is she at school?"

Sandra held her perfectly still for a moment. Then she pulled back, her face arranged in a neutral expression. Her eyes searched Kate's face.

"What?" asked Kate. "What is it? Did she get into trouble or something? Oh hell Sandra, has she been awful? I'm so sorry for putting you through this."

"It's not that." Sandra looked down at the space between them.

"What, then?" Kate felt her body turn cold. "Is it Robert? Did he come back?"

"No. Not Robert."

"What, then?"

She recalled the look on Sasha's face, the night she had kicked Robert out. Vulnerable, scared.

"Did she say anything to you?" she asked. "About Robert?"

Sandra shook her head. "Kate, this isn't about Robert. It's Julian."

"Julian?" Kate frowned. "Did he come visit her? Good.

He never gives her enough time since he took up with that Monique bitch."

"He's got her, Kate."

"He's with her now?"

"He came for her. Took her from the school. He's still on their approved list."

"So where are they?" It had been eighteen months since Julian, her ex-husband, had spent time alone with his daughter. "He'll have taken her somewhere too babyish. She'll hate it."

"He took her to California."

Kate felt like Sandra had punched her in the gut. "California."

"Three days ago. I'm sorry. He took her out of school and put her on a flight. She's gone, Kate."

CHAPTER TWENTY-EIGHT

Maya's body ached all over. The worst was her head, a pain behind her eyes that felt as if they were drilling their way out from her skull. The back of her neck screamed at her. It hurt even to blink.

She knew that her face was a mess. She'd tentatively raised a hand to her face after waking up and found bandages where she had expected cuts and bruises. When she prodded at them, it felt like her flesh was hollow beneath.

She lay back against the pillows, focusing on holding her aching limbs still. Her stomach hurt, a dull ache that would morph into sharp pain when she shifted position in the bed. This bed was narrow and uncomfortable. She had to tense herself to keep from falling out.

A young man in a white coat appeared at the end of the bed. He had thick black hair and a small snake tattoo poking up from the collar of his shirt. He grabbed the clipboard from the end of her bed, not making eye contact.

"Are you a doctor?" she asked.

He looked up, startled. "I didn't know you were awake."

She nodded her head, regretting it. She closed her eyes against the pain. He put down the clipboard and approached her.

"How do you feel?" He put a hand on her arm, his thumb brushing the tube that connected to the back of her hand. She grimaced.

"Bad."

"You were lucky," he told her. "You got hit on the head with something solid."

"A pipe," she whispered. She could see it now when she closed her eyes, swinging at her in the darkness.

"That figures," he said. "It could have been worse. They missed the important bits."

It didn't feel like they'd missed anything. "Did the cops come? What about the other woman? Is she OK?"

"What other woman?"

"There was a woman at the bus stop. They were giving her trouble."

"And you decided to step in?"

"I'm a doctor." Her throat felt tight. "Instinct."

His face softened at the news she was a fellow professional. "I'm Dr Yallopp. Here's the deal. You had concussion, but there's no serious damage. We'll have to keep you in here for observation for another twenty-four hours and then you can go home."

She closed her eyes. "Dr Yallop, tell me. Was I sexually assaulted?"

He flushed. "No. Just the head wound."

She nodded. The cops had got there in time, then.

"Do you have someone who can take care of you?" he asked.

"No."

"No family nearby? A neighbor?"

"I guess Mrs Rees might help out." She'd already asked enough favors of her neighbor, a shift worker with three kids and a lazy husband. She didn't relish the thought of adding to the woman's workload.

Dr Yallopp turned as another staff member approached. A heavyset white woman with wispy hair. She smiled at Maya as she leaned in to speak to the doctor.

Dr Yallopp turned to her. "You have a visitor."

"Who?"

He shrugged. "No idea. But you're in luck. Visiting doesn't end for another hour. You up for this?"

She wasn't up for conversation with anyone. But she was intrigued.

"Yes."

"Take it easy, huh? If it gets too much, tell them I said you needed time to recover."

"I will."

She slumped back as the doctor retreated. Exchanging a few words with him made her feel like she'd run a marathon. She hoped her visitor was someone who wouldn't expect to talk.

"Hey." A woman stood next to the bed, shifting from foot to foot. She had a yellowing bruise on her cheek and a bandage on her wrist.

"Er, hey."

The woman looked disappointed. "You don't remember me, do you?"

"I'm sorry. I had a bang to the head. I don't remember much." Maya's voice was thin; it was an effort to speak.

"I just wanted to say thank you, is all."

"OK."

"You might have saved my life back there."

The woman wore a red coat that was scuffed at the

collar. Her hair was curly and disheveled; she looked like she'd slept in her clothes.

"You're the woman at the bus stop."

"If you hadn't been there, I don't know what I woulda done."

"Right." Maya had no idea what else to say.

"Are you hurt?" Maya asked. "They hit you too."

"They tried."

The woman cast about her. "D'you mind if I sit? I haven't slept since yesterday morning."

Maya nodded her approval and the woman grabbed a chair and slid it up to the bed. "Thanks. The cops arrived just after they got you with that pipe. I was trying to run, but one of them grabbed me. Did this." She touched her cheek. "But I was lucky. You got it worse."

"I'm glad you're OK."

"I feel bad, you getting hurt like that."

"What's your name?"

"Fran."

"Fran. I'm Maya."

"Hey, Maya."

Maya took a few deep breaths. She felt sleep tug at her. She didn't want to make friends with this woman who'd just been in the wrong place at the wrong time.

"You're some sort of hero, you know," Fran said.

"No." Maya wanted to say more but it hurt too much. The throbbing at the back of her head was intensifying.

"You are. You stood up to those guys, even though they were bigger than you. I was terrified. I never coulda done that."

"I'm sure you could."

"Uh-uh. You should have a badge."

"I do. Sort of."

"You a cop?"

"A doctor."

"I bet you're a damn good doctor. You work here?"

Maya shook her head, just a little. Her throat hurt.

"No? Where you work then?"

"Nowhere you'd know." She didn't want to talk about her job; and besides, she might not have one anymore.

"Well, I say your patients are lucky. I hope you're my doctor someday."

"No, you don't."

The woman looked puzzled. Maya smiled. Her legs felt heavy and her eyelids were dropping. Had they given her a sedative?

"You look tired. I'd best be going." Fran pushed something into Maya's hand. "Here's my card. I work at Wells Fargo. If you ever need a loan, I'm your gal."

Maya smiled again, weakly. She might just need financial help, if things went badly at work.

"Thank you again. You have no idea how grateful I am. I hope you're feeling better very soon."

"Thanks."

Fran pushed the chair back. She leaned over Maya and gave her the lightest of kisses on the forehead. Maya waited for it to be over, feeling uneasy.

"See you around."

Maya listened to the woman's footsteps receding. They were soon replaced by the sounds of the ward: monitors buzzing, doctors murmuring to their patients, family members visiting. She heard a small child cry out.

As sleep washed over her, she wondered how on earth she was going to get her job back when she was stuck in the hospital.

CHAPTER TWENTY-NINE

"Hey, kid. Time to get up."

Cindee groaned and rubbed her eyes. She hated it when her mom woke her.

"Come on. Breakfast in ten."

She opened her eyes. She wasn't at home in bed, listening out for signs of her dad leaving for the day. She was in prison.

She sat up. Her legs felt heavy.

"You don't look so good today." Dora was pulling on a hoody, tying back her hair.

Cindee said nothing.

"I don't bite, you know. You can talk to me."

Cindee looked down at her feet. She was wearing two pairs of socks; it got cold here at night. She was already dressed. She turned to her bunk and dragged the sheet and blanket across it, making sure she tucked everything in neatly. She felt like she was wading through treacle.

"Wanna walk together?"

Cindee shook her head. Dora was being kind, she knew.

But she couldn't deal with kindness right now. She waved a dismissive hand and headed out.

The corridors were cold and damp. Cindee prowled towards the chow hall, trying not to make eye contact with anyone. She was tired and her stomach hurt. She'd had an appointment with the new doctor the day before, a check up on her baby. He'd poked and prodded, not caring that she was a human being too. To him, she was the incubator for the life inside her, no more.

She turned a corner to see a group of women standing in the space ahead of her, blocking her way. She hesitated then pulled back. These women were loud and confident, no doubt here for longer than she'd been, and they scared her. She stumbled backwards into a woman who was walking behind her.

"Hey! Watch where you're going."

"Sorry."

The woman looked her up and down, her gaze landing on Cindee's growing belly. The rest of her had become so thin that her belly made her look like some kind of freak, like she'd shoved a balloon up her sweater. She bit her lip—she was getting sores—and dodged the woman, heading back the way she had come.

She was pretty sure there was a route she could take around her old dorm that would lead her to the other end of the chow hall. It led past the kitchens, a noisy, bustling place she preferred to avoid. But today she was feeling like a small creature, unable to face other people. And she was hungry for once, or maybe the baby was.

She passed the turning that led back to her own cell and carried on walking. The flow of traffic was against her, women noisily making their way to breakfast. She wondered if there was a way through here, or if she'd been imagining things. Maybe there was, but it was out of bounds.

She turned a corner and stopped. A group of COs was up ahead, gathered around a doorway. They looked agitated. Another CO appeared from behind them and pushed through.

"Oh, hell," he said, not bothering to keep his voice down. "Now we're for it."

The hallway was emptying out, women pushing past her to get to their food. She stood staring at the officers, unable to move.

A man in a suit appeared. He had thin, graying hair and skin that looked like it might peel off at any moment.

"Who is it?" he barked.

One of the COs turned to him. She was pale. "Adams."

Cindee felt ice flow through her. She turned to run away.

The CO who had said her name spotted her. "Hey, you! You shouldn't be down here."

Cindee stared back at her, her heart racing. The guard hadn't recognized her. Which meant it hadn't been her she was talking about.

She took a step forward.

"Stop right there!" The guard advanced on her, her hand going to her belt. "Now turn around and go get your food. Like a good girl."

Cindee swallowed. "What's happened?" she asked.

"None o' your business."

Another CO came up behind the first one and tapped her shoulder. "We need as many of us in there as possible, to haul her out."

"Haul who out?" Cindee asked. "Suze?"

The first CO's cheeks reddened. "Who are you?"

"Cindee Adams."

The CO pushed out a sigh. "Shit." She turned to her colleague. "Get this one away from here, will you. It's her goddamn sister."

"Is she in there? Is she OK?" Cindee's legs were weakening. "Why do you need to haul her out?"

She pushed past the guards, not caring how much trouble she was going to get into. She didn't stop until she reached the doorway. Inside was full of bodies. Men and women in uniform, and one prisoner, on the floor. Her sister.

Cindee shrieked. She felt hands on her arms.

"Hey, stop that. Or we'll put you in solitary."

"Is she hurt?"

No answer.

"That's my sister. Is she hurt?" She felt her legs slacken. "Is she dead?"

Suze lay on the floor, not moving. Her skin was grey, and her legs lay at a crooked angle, as if she'd fallen.

"What happened?" Cindee cried. She yanked her arms out of the COs' grip. "Tell me!"

"Hernadez, you see to this." The man in the suit was talking. "Get her somewhere she can't cause any trouble. Tell her the bare minimum."

A female guard turned to her, trying to smile. Cindee scowled back at her. "She needs me. She needs my help. Let me go to her."

"I'm sorry," the CO—Hernandez—said. "Let us do our job."

Heat rose in her belly. Was that the baby moving? "Tell me what happened, please."

Hernandez steered her away from the doorway, back in the direction she had come. "She's taken an overdose. That's all I'm telling you. But you need to come with me. Tell me what you know."

"What *I* know? You think I had something to do with this?"

"We have to explore all the possibilities."

"Someone was hurting her. Someone she didn't want to tell me about. Talk to *them*."

"You're wrong. She did this to herself." The CO's face was pale.

"That's impossible." If you were given meds in this place, you had to swallow them in front of the guards.

"I can't talk to you about that. Now you come with me, and we can have a talk."

Cindee didn't want to talk. She wanted to run to Suze, to pump life back into her like Suze had with her when she'd taken those pills in the family bathroom, when she'd tried to get rid of this baby.

"She can't die. She can't."

CHAPTER THIRTY

"Who's this, then?"

"Grace Williams. Trial date next week." The CO accompanying Grace sounded bored.

The woman at the desk looked up. She had high cheekbones and thin eyebrows. She cocked her head at Grace. "You're the one killed your baby."

Grace tightened her jaw. She knew better than to answer back. The time to tell them what really happened would be in the courtroom.

"Huh. Not saying anything. Figures." The woman slapped a file shut and rose from her chair. She looked at the other guard. "Follow me."

Grace shuffled behind the two guards. She'd been shackled for the journey, a belt fastened around her waist, cuffs on her wrists and ankles. The skin on her leg was burning.

They passed six cells. In one, a man muttered to himself in the corner; in another, two women lay on benches staring up at the ceiling. The other cells held groups of men. As she passed the sixth, a man rushed at the bars. "Phew!" he whistled. "Fresh meat."

She sniffed, resisting the urge to look at him.

"Get back, Connor," the high-cheeked woman snapped. He laughed and staggered back to the floor, stumbling and landing in a tangle of limbs. Grace felt a shudder travel through her.

"Here we are." The woman stopped at a cell door. She nodded to the guard, who unfastened Grace's leg irons. Grace clenched and unclenched her toes and wriggled her ankles, glad of the freedom to move.

"Inside," the woman snapped. Grace held out her arms, expecting the handcuffs to be taken off.

"In a minute," the woman said.

Grace went inside and turned to face them. The door was locked, metal scraping on metal as it banged shut.

"Put your hands through."

Grace did as she was told, placing her hands on a shelf in the door. There was a slit large enough for her to reach through.

"No funny business." The woman unlocked her cuffs and drew them out. They rattled.

Grace pulled her hands back inside and rubbed her wrists. There were red weals where the metal had rubbed against her skin during the journey. She had no idea where she was or what route they'd taken; the roads had been unfamiliar and it had been all she could do to focus on not vomiting, the way the prison van was driven. She eased herself down on the thin bench that stood against one wall, opposite a toilet and sink. The cell smelt of sweat, vomit and Clorox.

A pair of eyes appeared at the hatch in the door. "Food will be around in an hour or so. If you're lucky."

Grace nodded. She hadn't eaten since yesterday; it had been just gone dawn when they'd woken her and told her to move out. There had been no warning; she knew her trial date was coming up but hadn't been told when it was or when she would be moved to the county jail. She guessed it was time.

She wondered when she would meet the public defender. She needed someone who knew what they were doing. But she didn't need charity, she didn't need that WASPy Kate woman sticking her nose in where it wasn't wanted. She'd find a way, somehow.

"Hey!"

She ignored the voice; it was high-pitched, a woman.

"I say hey!"

She approached the door to her cell, wondering if the *hey* had been for her. Was it one of the staff, or another inmate?

"You just been arrested?"

The accent was familiar. She drew in a shaky breath. "No."

"No? What ya doin' here then?"

"Waiting for trial." She wished she hadn't answered now. The woman would want to know what she was on trial for. What her chances were.

"When?"

That wasn't so bad. "Next week, they tell me."

"You been on remand long?"

"Just a few weeks. What about you?"

"Oh, I'll be outta here tomorrow. My man's gonna post bail."

Lucky you, thought Grace. She thought of Linton, in jail himself. She didn't even know if he'd had his trial yet.

"Can I ask you something?"

136

"Course you can."

"You from Houston?"

"Yeah, South Park. What about you, sister?"

"Yeah."

"That makes us neighbors. Pleased to meet you. I'm Shana."

"Hey, Shana." Grace wondered if the other prisoners were listening. She lowered her voice. "You been here long?"

"One night. This time, anyways."

Grace moved towards the wall that separated their cells, keeping close to the bars. "Shana?"

"Yeah?"

"I didn't suppose you know of a Linton Williams, do you?"

"Linton Williams?"

Grace felt herself hollow out. She shouldn't have said his name. That was a mistake.

"Yes, I do believe I do. My man works with his brother, Charlie Williams. That the one? Work at the warehouse on MLK Boulevard?"

"He did." Until he was arrested for stealing stock. He hadn't even been on shift that night, but they needed someone to blame and he fit the profile: tall, slim, black. "You heard anything about him?"

There was a pause. Grace wondered if the woman had heard her. Or if she'd stepped out of line.

"I'm sorry, sister."

Grace slumped against the door. "Why?"

"His trial was put back again, or so Waylan told me. Disgrace, it is. Everyone knows he didn't do nothin'."

No, thought Grace. *Linton did nothing*. Unless turning up for work every day and working your butt off for an employer who didn't give a damn for you was nothing.

"Thanks." She didn't want to talk about it. All she knew was she had to get out of here, for her kids' sake. Linton would be out of the picture for a good while, if she knew the Texas justice system.

She moved away from the door.

"You alright there, friend?"

"I'm OK. Thank you."

"I'm sorry to be the bearer of bad news."

Grace nodded. She couldn't speak; her throat was tight, and tears rolled down her cheek. She thought of Boo, the way he'd called for the ambulance when she'd been having the miscarriage. Sissy, the scared look in her eyes. And Charlie, her big boy. Vee next door couldn't be expected to take care of them forever.

But she'd rejected the only person who'd offered her help. She had a lawyer who'd most likely never defended a case like hers. And she lived in a country that despised women like her.

She lay down on the bench and let the tears fall freely.

CHAPTER THIRTY-ONE

KATE PERSUADED SANDRA TO TAKE HER HOME; THERE
was a chance Sasha might be there.

She fumbled in the Ziploc bag she'd been issued for her
belongings and pulled out her keys.

"Should you be here?" asked Sandra. "I thought I was
supposed to take you to that halfway house."

"We'll go there next," Kate replied. "This is more
important."

She pushed open the front door. The house felt musty.
She could smell rotting fruit.

"Sasha?"

No response. She dropped her bag and ran through the
house, throwing open doors, going onto closets. Sasha's
room was empty.

"He's taken her things."

Sandra entered the room, breathing heavily. She was
short and stout, with legs that were unused to dashing
around like this. "Son of a bitch."

"Her closet is empty. No clothes. Her laptop is gone.

Books, shoes." She sat heavily on the bed. "Oh God, Sandra. She's gone."

Sandra put a hand on her arm and sat next to her. "We'll get her back."

"Will we? I'm an ex-con. I had an abortion. What kind of mother do you think a family court will take me for?"

"You're a damn good mom, Kate. You know it, and Sasha knows it. Julian doesn't have a leg to stand on."

"I hope so."

She heaved herself up and went to Sasha's dresser. Her passport was gone, and her ebony necklace, the one Julian's mother had given her before she died.

"She had time to do this properly. He planned this."

"He took advantage."

Kate shook her head. "He was planning it all along, the bastard. He didn't care about her when he left me for that Monique woman, but now when I'm vulnerable, he pounces."

"We'll fight him, Kate. I'm a family lawyer, remember? I know what to do."

"I know enough about the law to know that a woman who's just come out of jail won't be looked on too favorably in a custody battle. I shouldn't even be here; I'm supposed to be at the halfway house."

Sandra stood up. "Yeah. We need to get you there pronto. The less time you spend here, the better."

"Can I just get my things?"

"You can't turn up there with things you clearly got from home. No, let me come back later. I'll make up a bag for you, and bring it in."

Kate nodded. She opened another drawer, to find Sasha's pencil case missing. She rubbed her temples.

"You need to keep your head, Kate. Stick to the rules

and show that you're to be trusted. Tell me what you need me to bring, and I'll do it. Then I'll go into the office and start on your case."

"You've got enough cases already. They won't let you—"

"Kate. We look after our own. I'll persuade Tom Abad to let me take your case. He let me work for Tasha Bains when she was going through a messy divorce. Not that I ever told you that."

"This is different."

"I'll get Sasha back for you, Kate. You just sit tight at the halfway house for the two weeks you're supposed to, and it'll work out fine."

"I damn well hope so."

"Come on. We need to get moving."

Kate followed Sandra downstairs. She turned off the light as she left Sasha's room, hoping none of the neighbors had spotted her. Mrs Evans next door was friendly enough, but there was a young guy across the street who had always looked at her funny.

A pile of letters lay on the mat. She stared at it.

"Don't touch it," Sandra said. "You haven't been here, remember?"

"I know." One of the letters caught Kate's eye; it was from her landlord.

"That one is important."

Sandra sighed. "I'll bring you the rest when I come with your things. I'll come in here every few days, check your post, open and close the curtains for you. Do your neighbors know where you've been?'

Kate picked it up carefully, not touching the rest of the pile. "I have no idea. But I guess it wasn't a secret that I was convicted."

"Let's hope they haven't spotted us." Sandra opened the

front door and ushered Kate out, glancing from left to right. If Kate hadn't been feeling so numb, she might have found it funny.

They got into the car in silence and drove away, Sandra taking care to drive smoothly and not draw attention. Kate opened the letter she'd been clutching in her lap.

"Oh, hell."

Sandra hesitated before pulling out of a junction. "What is it?"

"The landlord. I'm in breach of contract."

"You're what?" Sandra looked over at the letter then pulled her eyes back to the road.

Kate frowned. "They say I'm in breach of a morality clause."

"A *what*?"

"Oh, hell. It's one of those blanket clauses, designed to catch unsavory types."

"You're not an unsavory type."

"According to them, I am."

"What can they do about it?"

"This says they sent me another letter, a month earlier. I didn't reply."

"That's absurd. How could you reply when you were in prison?"

"I don't think that helps me any, Sandra."

"What are they doing to do?"

"They've given me a fortnight. Then they're evicting me."

"That's when you're due to leave the halfway house."

"It is. And if I don't have a home to go to, how can I fight Julian and get Sasha back?"

CHAPTER THIRTY-TWO

Cindee pushed past the CO, suddenly stronger than her hundred-pound frame.

"I don't believe you!"

"Hey, inmate. Stop right there." She felt a hand on her arm, pulling her back. More hands landed on her, tugging at her, grabbing her. She yanked out of their grip, full of anger.

"Let me see her!"

One of the COs snapped cuffs onto her and another grabbed the back of her shirt. She struggled in their grip, not caring about being a good girl anymore.

Two more guards arrived, carrying a stretcher. She screamed. She pulled against the restraints, yelling. Then she felt pressure in the small of her back and she was on the ground, face down, a CO's knee on her back.

"Stay right where you are. I don't want to hurt you."

Cindee didn't care. "I have to see my sister."

"You have to behave yourself, is what you have to do."

The guard's breath was hot in her ear. "Behave yourself, or you'll wind up in solitary."

She tensed against the woman's grip but she wasn't

strong enough. There were three of them on her now; the one at her back, one at her head and another who had hold of her feet. She felt the strength seep out of her.

There was muttering among the guards and she saw a pair of feet passing. They weren't wearing the heavy black boots that the COs wore, but a pair of brown leather shoes that looked recently polished.

"What's going on?"

"It's Adams, Doctor. She OD'd." The CO sounded uneasy.

Cindee struggled again, hoping the arrival of the doctor would distract them. The CO with her knee in Cindee's back pulled her upright.

"Move. You've caused enough trouble."

The doctor turned to them. It was the same doctor she'd had for the first time last week, the one with the expensive suit and eyes that looked straight through you. "Who's this?"

"The girl's sister."

The doctor frowned. "Sister, huh?" He looked at Cindee, his eyes cold. "She tell you she was going to do this?"

Cindee said nothing.

"Mute, are you? Stupid girls. Your own worst enemy."

"Sorry, Dr Abbott, but we need to take her away."

"I just want to see her," Cindee said.

The doctor smiled. "Not so silent after all?" He put his fingers on her chin and raised it. "Hmmm. Prettier than your sister. Are you one of mine?"

She said nothing, but gritted her teeth, biting in the anger.

"Not going to tell me?" He smiled. "I can check my records."

He turned to the CO. "Don't punish her." He licked his lips; they were thin and pale. He had short dark hair and eyes that were almost black. If he hadn't been so creepy, he'd be good-looking. Cindee had a sudden thought of her father. She shivered.

"She's had a shock," he continued. "She needs our compassion." He cocked his head at her. "Come and see me tomorrow, huh? I'll book you a session. You'll need medical help, after all this."

She stared back at him, feeling her chest tighten. "I want to see her."

"I don't think that would be appropriate. We don't want to give you any ideas."

He stroked her chin. She forced her hand to stay at her side, despite the urge to bat him away.

"Take her back to her cell," he said. "I'll see her tomorrow."

CHAPTER THIRTY-THREE

It felt strange to wear a suit again. Kate straightened her jacket as she got out of the cab and looked up at the building she'd worked in for the last three years. Her office was on a corner on the thirteenth floor; she had a great view of downtown Austin.

She leaned back into the cab to hand the driver a tip, once again marveling at how strange it felt to be doing things like riding in cars and wearing suits after her time in jail. Had it been only two days ago she'd been wearing prison-issue khakis and eating the slop they served up in the chow hall?

Her suit felt loose, of course; the enforced prison diet, even for two months, had seen the pounds slide off. It did no harm; she'd been meaning to lose weight. Sandra brought her clothes within hours of dropping her at the halfway house: two cases of office wear and jeans, plus a box of books and other personal effects. And another full of case files. "No harm in hitting the ground running," she'd said, urging Kate to focus on her own job while she, Sandra, took on the job of getting Sasha back.

She took a deep breath and patted her hair before pushing through the revolving door into the building. The lobby was warm, decorated with a vast Christmas tree. Was it Christmas, already? She thought of Sasha, the traditions they'd built up together in the two years since Julian had left. What would Christmas be like in the desert, she wondered? Then she shook her head. Sasha would be back before Christmas. Of course she would.

She swiped her card through the reader and said hello to Carl, the security guard. He looked at her askance but didn't say anything about the fact that she'd been missing two months. Did he know where she'd been?

She rode the elevator in silence, not recognizing any of the people in there with her. At the thirteenth floor she and a young man she didn't recognize got out. She nodded at him. She was a senior partner; although they hadn't met, he would know who she was. She felt her chest clench just a little, wondering what the other partners had told the staff about her absence.

She headed for her office at the corner of the building. As she passed colleagues, they paused to glance at her, then carried on with their business. She'd been expecting a warmer welcome. But maybe being ignored, or almost ignored, was preferable. Maybe she just needed to pick up as if she'd never been away.

She arrived at her office. A slender Asian woman was sitting at the desk outside; not Shona, her brash but reliable Irish assistant.

"Hello?" Kate said. "Who are you?"

The woman stood up. She looked uneasy. "My name is Lin," she said. She rubbed her palm on her skirt—designer, Kate noted—and held it out. "You must be Ms Mitchell."

She ignored the hand. "Where's Shona? Is she sick?"

"Errr…" Lin looked into Kate's office. Sitting inside, in her own chair, with his back to them, was Claude White, one of the named partners.

Kate twisted her lips. She and Claude had never been close; why had he been chosen as her welcoming party? "Thank you," she told Lin, and pushed through the glass doors. Hopefully Claude would tell her what had happened to Shona.

"Claude, hi," she said, keeping her voice as light as she could. He swiveled round to face her, a stiff smile on his face.

"Kate. How are you?"

"I'm great, thank you. Ready to get back to work."

"Yes."

"Do you know where Shona is?"

He licked his lips. "We had to let her go, I'm afraid."

"But she's the best secretary we have."

He raised an eyebrow. "One of the best, perhaps. But we no longer needed her."

"Why not? Why have you given me a new assistant? And why wasn't I involved in hiring this Lin woman?"

He stood up and leaned on the desk between them. He sniffed. "Kate. You didn't expect to just waltz in here and have things pick up exactly as you left them, did you?"

She stared at him. "I appreciate you holding my job open." She considered mentioning Josh passing her case to an associate then decided against it. "I've only been gone two months. I can make up the time, I assure you."

He leaned forward. "It's not that."

"What, then?"

"It doesn't look good for the firm."

She was ready for this. She'd done her research; or

rather, Sandra had. "I'm not the first partner who's come back after a conviction. Brian Morston in 1997, he—"

Claude raised a hand to stop her. "That was different."

"He spent three months in jail. He came straight back to work. I think that, and the fact you're letting me come back, demonstrates how much value you place in your team, and the importance of retaining experienced staff."

He snorted. "You broke the law, Kate. We have a reputation to uphold."

"I pled guilty. My crime had no bearing on my ability as a lawyer, or my right to continue to practice."

"It's not just about the law. It's about a certain set of moral standards."

"Claude. This is a socially progressive firm. Between the partners and associates, we did a thousand hours of pro bono work last year. Surely you aren't—"

"We are, Kate. I'm afraid we've had clients express concern. Two of them have said they will leave us if we allow you to stay on at the firm."

"You're firing me."

"Letting you go. We'll buy out your partnership at a generous rate, I assure you."

"I bet you will."

"What's that supposed to mean?"

"Nothing. Give me a chance, Claude. I'm a damn good lawyer. You know I won't find a job with another firm if you fire me."

"That can't be our concern, I'm afraid."

"Where are the other named partners? Amanda and Tom? Why aren't they here, looking me in the eye? Or was this all your idea?"

"We're unanimous in this decision. I wouldn't be here if we weren't."

I bet, thought Kate. Tom Abad had hired her as an associate when she was fresh out of college; he'd been her mentor, he'd steered her rise to her current level. He'd hinted that she might make named partner herself within a couple of years. Had he really agreed to this, or had he been outvoted?

"I want to speak to Tom."

"He's out of state right now, on client business."

How convenient. "I'll find him. He'll see my side."

"I'm sorry, Kate, but he won't. I was on the phone to him before you came in."

She stared at him, fire raging in her chest. Her daughter, her house, and now her job. Was there going to be anything left?

Claude looked at his watch. "You have twenty minutes, after which I expect you to be out of the building. Lin will help you to identify what in here belongs to you, and what to the firm. Please make sure you don't take anything that isn't yours."

He stood for a moment, his hand hovering in front of him, then thought better and withdrew it. He gave her a curt nod and left the room. She watched him stride along the hallway, leaving a sea of colleagues in his wake, all of them staring past him and toward her.

CHAPTER THIRTY-FOUR

Kate wasn't accustomed to being alone in the daytime. Like all lawyers, she worked long hours and rarely got home before darkness, especially at this time of year.

She approached the halfway house, wondering who else would be inside. She'd barely spoken to the other women last night; there were three more on her floor, and they'd grunted at her as she'd arrived. She was going to be here no more than two weeks if her lawyer did his job; it hardly seemed worth making friends.

Maybe she would have to, now.

She took a deep breath and forced herself up the path leading to the front door. The paint was peeling in places, revealing a coat of white paint under the blue. She wondered how often this place was maintained.

They didn't trust the women with actual keys, too easy to lose or to sell. Each of them had their own individual code, so if one was used to enter the house illicitly, the authorities would know who to blame.

She lifted the cover over the keypad and punched in her code, shivering. The sky was gray, and it looked like rain.

She sniffed as she shouldered the door aside and bundled herself into the hallway.

The hallway was large, not unusual for a house like this, one of Austin's rare historic buildings. In the right neighborhood and with the right interior designer, it would be worth a fortune.

She went to shrug off her coat then stopped herself. There were no hooks here, no messily strewn shoes and bags like she'd complained about so many times with Sasha and, at one time, Julian. Instead, the hallway was bare, the only signs of life a small pile of post on the narrow console table. She picked it up, hesitantly, and rifled through. Nothing for her.

There was a common room on this floor, a large space with a bay window overlooking the street. She didn't feel like retreating to the confines of her own musty room right now; maybe some company would do her good.

She went to the door and raised a hand to knock, then dropped it. She had as much right to be here as anyone. She pushed her way inside.

The room was empty of people. A large, pockmarked coffee table sat in the center of a threadbare Persian rug, littered with dirty mugs and cigarette butts. Around it was a mismatched set of aging armchairs and a large TV that dominated the corner of the room.

She slumped onto the least dingy-looking of the chairs and looked around. The room smelt of cigarette smoke mixed with sweat and the faint aroma of Thai food. She hadn't eaten here yet: would she use the kitchen, or was bringing back takeout allowed?

On the table immediately in front of her was a remote control. She leaned over to pick it up and flicked the TV on. She pulled off her coat and draped it over the arm of her chair. She would need to get up and put it in her room. She would need to change into more comfortable clothes. There were lots of things she needed to do, but right now all she could do was sit.

She flicked through the channels. Daytime TV: *Jeopardy*, a talk show on dangerous dogs, news channels. She'd tried to catch the news when she could on the prison TV set but the other inmates had complained; it wasn't something they wanted to know about. So she was hungry to find out what had been happening in her absence.

She alighted on a local news channel. She tossed the remote back onto the table, holding her breath at the clatter it made and looking at the door. No one appeared.

She let the news dance in front of her eyes, barely registering. Some scandal in the mayor's office. A local school being closed down for fumigation after rats were found in the Kindergarten classroom. Then the story switched to a woman being put on trial for murder.

She leaned forward. She knew that woman.

She held her breath as the camera followed the jumpsuit-clad woman being led from an unmarked van to the Travis County Courthouse. A cop had his hand up to shield her face, but she was still recognizable. Kate worked at that courthouse regularly; she'd been expecting to be back there today. Would she have seen Grace, if she had?

She stood and approached the TV. The volume was low; she was too agitated to think about grabbing the remote.

"The woman, who we can't name for legal reasons, is on trial for killing her late-term baby," the newswoman explained. "It's the first case of its kind in Texas and it's attracting a lot of attention."

A flash popped onscreen and Grace turned towards it,

squinting. She looked tired; her eyes were shadowed and her skin sallow. Kate wondered what kind of representation a woman from South Park with three kids and a husband on remand would be able to afford. The court-appointed lawyer, no doubt.

The camera panned out to reveal a jostling crowd. Grim-faced people holding boards that depicted mutilated fetuses and slogans about divine retribution were faced by a younger, quieter crowd of women holding pro-choice placards. *Repeal AVA. Right to Choose. Respect Women.*

The camera shifted to follow Grace as she was pushed into the courthouse. They'd brought her in via the front entrance, something they only did when they wanted to make an example of a prisoner.

Kate thought of Grace's face when they'd met in their cell. Of the weariness and exasperation. The miscommunication. *I think you've misjudged me.*

There was a yell—*Murderer*—as the police officer put a hand on Grace's shoulder to push her further inside. Grace turned momentarily, her eyes wide, her mouth open.

Kate grabbed the remote. She raced through the channels, seeking out more information, better coverage. But there was nothing, not yet at least.

She had to know more. She had to do something.

She dropped the remote and grabbed her coat, then almost dropped it again when she heard the door behind her open and close. Two women had joined her; both black, both way younger than her.

They stopped mid-conversation and stared at her. "You must be the new girl," one of them said. She wore purple eyeliner and had a tattoo of a bird on her wrist.

"Uh, yeah," Kate replied. "Sorry."

She pushed past the women and out of the door.

"Where you goin'?" The woman called after her.

"Nowhere!"

She paused in the hallway. Would this put Sasha at risk? Could what she was about to do mean her daughter was taken away from her?

If she went back in there, she was giving up. She was letting them win. That wasn't the woman she wanted her daughter to emulate.

She shook her head, cursing herself, and then pushed open the front door.

CHAPTER THIRTY-FIVE

THE COURTHOUSE FELT AT ONCE FAMILIAR AND ALIEN.

Kate hurried up the steps, avoiding the eyes of the sharp-suited lawyers passing her in the opposite direction. It was 1pm and most courtrooms would be breaking for recess. Time to grab some lunch, bone up on case files, or brief your client.

She pulled the heavy wooden doors open and stepped inside, closing her eyes for a second to absorb the familiar smells. The heavy scent of wood paneling, mingling with the freshly ground coffee beans wafting down from the coffee shop at the top of the stairs, and the occasional flash of mustiness as a homeless person passed. Since the passing of the Vagrancy Act, so many homeless people were the subjects of criminal cases that the courthouse had become a kind of refuge for people who had nowhere to go. It was easy to pass yourself off as just another down-and-out defendant, and the staff were reluctant to check. A man snored on a bench behind her and a woman sat on the floor in a corner, surrounded by bags. Kate wondered why she'd never paid them any attention before.

The clerk at the main desk was a tough-talking older woman called Ms Thomson; the lawyers had spent the last ten years wondering if she'd ever take retirement.

Kate approached her, plastering on her broadest and most confident smile. She was glad she was still in her office clothes but wished she'd thought to grab a briefcase as armor.

"Hey, Ms Thomson, how are you today?"

The woman looked up over thick black-rimmed spectacles. "Why, if it isn't young Kate Mitchell, hotshot attorney-at-law."

Kate forced out a laugh. "The very same."

"Haven't seen you around here none lately." Ms Thomson tapped her pencil against the desk, her mouth downturned. She had one of the most onerous jobs in this building and was probably the only person who knew what the hell was happening any given day.

"I've been away."

"Hmmm."

Kate felt blood rise to her cheeks. Her own trial had been in another courthouse, one closer to the clinic, thank God. But still; nothing had been hidden and anyone might know exactly where she'd been 'away' to.

"Not for me to judge." Ms Thomson waved away a young man in a blue suit who was trying to push in front of Kate, barking out anxious questions. "What can I help you with, honey?"

"I'm working on a case. But because I've been away, I don't know which courtroom."

"Why, that's a little absent-minded of you."

"Sorry."

"You can't check with your assistant?"

Kate wasn't about to tell Ms Thomson she had no idea

where Shona was. Her assistant had dealt with Ms Thomson many times; delivering documents while Kate was deep into a trial, persuading her to put files in front of a judge at the last possible minute. Shona had an easy smile and a matter-of-fact manner that endeared her to the older woman.

"She's off sick."

"Poor girl. She seems strong as an ox to me. Ain't seen her lately, either."

"No. Anyway, the case."

"The case." She scratched her nose. A line was growing behind Kate but Ms Thomson clearly didn't care. "Which one is it you need me to look up for you?"

"People vs Grace Williams."

A raised eyebrow. "Didn't know that one had top-drawer representation."

"It does now."

"Good. She deserves all she can get, that poor girl."

Kate said nothing. A defendant's attorney was a matter of record and making changes when the case was already in session was frowned upon. Except, it seemed, today.

"Courtroom twelve. You know where it is, I assume?"

"I do."

"Good for you."

"Thanks. I appreciate it."

"Only doin' my job."

"Well, thanks."

Kate sped off toward courtroom twelve, glancing back to see Ms Thomson wink at her as the impatient young man leaned over her desk. She took the stairs two at a time, knowing the room she sought was as far away as it could be: upstairs, at the back. And that her reception when she got there would not be a warm one.

At the door to the courtroom she paused to smooth her hair and skirt, and to lick her lips. She had no idea if her lipstick was still in place. She would have to do.

She pushed open the doors as calmly as she could and walked inside, pasting a look of confidence onto her face.

Inside, the judge was staring blankly at a young attorney in a crumpled suit as he struggled through what seemed to be his opening statement. Grace sat at the table behind him, her head bowed. She wore the orange jumpsuit Kate had seen her in on TV. That would have to change, for a start.

Kate slid into a seat in the back row, smiling tightly at the juror who glanced up to frown at her. He nodded and turned back to watch the lawyer along with his colleagues.

The jury was made up of eight men and four women. Two of the men were black and one Asian. Only one of the women was black. They looked from the lawyer to Grace and back again repeatedly, forming their judgments of the orange-clad woman on trial.

Kate pushed down an urge to intervene and listened to the arguments being made. She needed to educate herself on how this case was being defended before she got involved. She needed to pick her moment.

"During the course of this trial, you will see for your-selves what kind of woman Grace Williams is. Devoted mother, hardworking teacher, loving wife. You will learn about the heartache she suffered when she learned that her baby was to be born with a serious heart defect. The conver-sation she had with her doctor about her choices. And her agony when she miscarried that child."

Choices. Conversation with her doctor. This wasn't the best approach. If that jury, that two-thirds male, two-thirds white jury was going to acquit Grace, they didn't need to be offered words like *choice* and *conversation.* They needed to know that Grace had had no choice. That she was a victim of a system that mistrusted women like her and plunged their children into chaos because of that mistrust.

And they needed a new jury. Six of them hadn't taken their eyes off Grace in the last two minutes. Five of those were men, and none of them looked sympathetic. One of the men, a tall, dark-haired guy with skin so pale he looked radioactive, was looking down his nose at Grace like he thought she was subhuman. That jumpsuit wouldn't be helping matters.

Kate stood up. She approached the front of the courtroom.

"Excuse me."

Judge Haynes, a silver-haired woman Kate had appeared in front of a few times, looked away from Grace's lawyer and at Kate. "Yes?"

Kate nodded in acknowledgement. "Your Honor. I apologize for the interruption. But there has been a material change in this case."

Judge Haynes pushed a stray hair aside. "And that would be?"

"The representing attorney, your Honor. I've been appointed as counsel in this case."

She avoided looking at Grace, who would be confused. Did Grace recognize her? Would she accept her help now, after she'd dismissed her before?

"Excuse me," the attorney said. He looked less than thirty, and his suit needed cleaning as well as pressing. He had dark hair, sandy brown skin and the look of someone you would trust but maybe not rely on. "I have no knowledge of this change."

"Ms Mitchell," said the judge. "I don't like being interrupted in my courtroom. Why didn't you tell me about this earlier?"

"Because I didn't know. I only just discovered that I'd been allocated this case."

"So this is now with White, Petersik and Abad?"

"It's with me. I'm representing Ms Williams privately."

The judge sighed. "In my chambers, now. Both of you, plus prosecuting counsel." She nodded at a heavy woman wearing a bright blue suit. Becca Lloyd, Assistant District Attorney and Kate's old enemy. She was good. With a mean streak as wide as the Mississippi.

"Of course, ma'am."

"That's enough of the ma'aming. You just explain this good, and we'll be alright."

Kate allowed herself a look at Grace as the lawyers stepped through the door at the back of the room. She was glaring at Kate. She didn't look happy.

CHAPTER THIRTY-SIX

Cindee entered the doctor's office, her skin shrinking the closer she got to him.

There was something about this doctor; an assuredness that made her feel anything but confident. He looked at her in a way that reminded her of her father. She clenched her teeth and squared her jaw, pushing away visions of his face, the way that lock of his hair used to move when he came to her at night.

Prison was terrifying to a girl like Cindee, raised soft and sheltered from the rougher elements of society. But at least there'd been one consolation: no visits from her family. She could deal with Mom abandoning her if it meant she wouldn't have to see *him*.

But now he'd been replaced, by this doctor. Who was staring at her right now as if he owned her. His head was cocked and he wore a smile that he probably thought was sincere but in reality was patronizing and creepy.

"So. Cindee," he smiled. "Take a seat."

She grabbed the chair which had been placed at right angles to his own, around the corner of the desk. As she did so, she pulled it back and away from him. She edged into it, tucking her feet beneath her and placing clenched hands in her lap.

He didn't lower his smile but leaned forward. His breath smelled of eggs. She struggled to breathe.

"How are you today? It was rough, what you had to go through yesterday."

Rough. If rough was how he described finding out that your sister had tried to kill herself in prison, then he'd never experienced anything like it. She kept her eyes down, staring at the blue tie he'd tucked into his shirt. It made him look childish.

"Talk to me, Cindee. I can't help you if you won't open up."

She raised her head, her jaw firm. "I'm OK."

"I don't think I'd be OK, in your shoes."

"I'm fine." She looked past him at a spot on the wall. It looked like someone had thrown a coffee cup at it; an uneven brown stain with a darker patch at its center. Maybe someone had. Maybe it had been their only way to get this guy away from them.

She shivered.

He placed a hand on her knee. She jerked back, the chair scraping loudly on the wooden floor. She stared down at the hand, paralyzed. She knew she should push it off. But he was a doctor and she a patient; he prison staff and she an inmate. No one would believe her, if he chose to accuse her of violence.

She tightened the muscles in her thigh and focused on the mark on the wall.

He smiled. "I hope I can help you, Cindee. You strike me as a bright girl. You've got a good future ahead of you."

She felt fluttering in her abdomen. She put a hand to it;

shush. Could she be losing it? Would they believe it wasn't her fault, if she did? She'd seen Grace, that woman who everyone said had aborted her sick fetus. Miscarriages didn't exist anymore. Not for people like her and Grace.

She moved her hand away from her stomach; best not to alert him.

"Now." He took his hand off of hers and she wriggled her fingers, trying out the freedom. "I need to examine you. You've had quite a shock. Best to be sure it hasn't affected your baby."

"I'm not due an ultrasound for another four weeks."

He cocked his head again, smiling. "Not an ultrasound. Not this time. I can do this by hand."

She stared at his hands. She felt very small, and utterly powerless. The room was moving away from her in the way it used to when her dad was around, making her feel as if she was shrinking into a corner.

"I'm fine," she croaked. "Don't need an exam."

"Nonsense." He stood up. He grabbed a bottle from the desk between them and tipped it into his palm, smearing pungent liquid over his hands. He snapped a pair of latex gloves out of a dispenser and tugged them on.

"Come on, then. Up on the couch."

She thought of the last time she'd lain on that couch, Dr Henderson's hands traveling around her abdomen. That had been bad enough, but this?

She pushed herself upright. Her feet wouldn't move.

"I don't have all day, you know."

She swallowed. The dark patch on the wall was growing, as if it might eat them up. She wondered what would happen if he fell into it. The room was swaying, or was it her?

"Here." He was next to her, his arm around her shoulder. How had he got there? "I'll guide you. You're clearly not well."

"I'm fine."

"I can't hear you, Cindee."

"I said..." her voice was gone. She opened her mouth, but nothing came out. She looked at the door. It wasn't locked, was it? She could run?

Her feet still wouldn't move.

"Come on." His voice was dark and fluid. He tugged at her shoulder, almost tipping her up.

At last her feet moved, skittering beneath her.

He half-dragged her to the couch against the wall. There was a roll of paper over it, just like there had been before. This was a doctor's office. She was a pregnant woman. She could do this.

She nodded slowly, then allowed him to guide her up to the couch. She sat on it and smoothed her hands on the paper.

"Lie down, Cindee." He was frowning.

"I'd rather sit." Her voice had come back, just a little. She congratulated herself.

"I need to check the baby. I can't do that while you're sitting there like an idiot."

More fluttering. "The baby's fine. I can feel it kicking."

"I'll need to check that."

"I can, honest." She put her hand on her stomach, scared of the thing inside her. "It's moving. It's fine."

He shook his head. "And you think you're qualified to give a medical opinion, do you?"

"I can feel it."

He put both hands on her shoulders. He pushed her lightly; when she resisted, he pushed harder. "Lie down, or I'll have to get a CO to restrain you."

RACHEL MCLEAN

"Go on then."

He raised an eyebrow. He laughed. "It bites."

"I don't need examining."

"You do. Stay there."

He went to the door and opened it, glancing back at her repeatedly. She watched him, working out her chances of escape. They were slim; she knew better than to move from this spot.

"I need you in here," he said to someone outside. Cindee felt a shiver run through her body.

She stared as a female CO entered behind the doctor. "No," she said. "I'm fine. I'll behave. I don't need restraining."

The doctor smiled at the guard. She was young, hard-faced. Gutierez, Cindee remembered her being called. "She's lying, of course," he said. "They all do. Refusing to be examined."

The CO rolled her eyes. "Come on then."

"No," said Cindee. "Please, don't."

"Too late for that." The doctor looked at her, his eyes dancing. "Officer, please ensure she can't move from the bed."

The CO frowned but brought a pair of handcuffs out from her belt. "I need to stay here, once I do this," she said.

"I'm her doctor," the doctor said. "This is confidential, between me and her. You can leave us."

"If an inmate is restrained..."

"Uh-uh. Not for medical purposes. Not since Congress passed AVA."

The American Values Amendment. Cindee's father had welcomed it. Her mother, a traditionalist, had too. Their preacher had spoken of its being sent down from God to confirm their church had been right all along.

166

Cindee had ignored it; politics wasn't her thing. It gave personhood to fetuses from the moment of conception, restricted mothers' right to work and, it seemed, dealt with prisoners too.

"Oh. Yeah. You're right." Officer Gutierez looked uneasy.

"Right," said the doctor. "So...?"

The guard placed the cuffs on Cindee's ankle, the other end attached to the bed. Cindee sat awkwardly, refusing to lie down. Her body twisted uncomfortably; she was squashing the baby.

"Thank you, Officer. I'll call you when the prisoner needs to be released."

"Please don't leave me with him," Cindee said.

The CO looked at her. "Shoulda thought of that before you refused to cooperate."

"He'll hurt me."

"Why would I do that?" The doctor's voice was smooth, like chocolate.

"I'll be right outside," said the CO. The doctor nodded and let her out, pushing the door firmly behind her. He yanked the drapes closed around the bed. The camera, up in the corner, was hidden from view.

"Now," he turned back to Cindee. "You lie down and behave yourself."

She stayed where she was, ignoring the pain in her stomach, the cuffs that chafed at her ankle.

He put a hand in the center of her chest and pushed. She fell back, her head hitting the wall.

She landed in a twisted position against the wall, her leg hanging over the end of the couch. He grabbed her under the arms and heaved her round, forcing her to lie straight. She felt sick. He pulled up her t-shirt and yanked her sweatpants halfway down her thighs. She threw her hand to her crotch.

"Stop it," he muttered. He shoved her hand out of the way. She yelped. He put one hand on the top of her stomach and another at the bottom. She held her breath.

He squeezed, hard. She let out a muffled cry. Her head was spinning and there was pain behind her eyes. She had to stay awake.

He squeezed again, then pulled his hands apart. He twisted them in the same way the other doctor had, assessing the way the baby was lying.

She bit her bottom lip, allowing herself to hope that he was just going to examine her after all.

He dug his fingertips into her flesh again, pushing the breath out of her. He was no longer wearing the gloves, and his skin was rough. He was panting, his head bowed towards her naked stomach.

She looked at the back of his head, wondering if she could knock him out. If she could bite him. But she was attached to this bed; what would she do after that?

He took his hands off her stomach. One hand moved swiftly down and grabbed her, hard, between the legs. She let out a cry.

He lifted his head to look at her. "That's a warning. You behave yourself from now on, and I won't have to restrain you."

She stared at him, mute. She nodded. Anything to get away from here, to get this man's hands off her.

He pulled back and rubbed his hands together, letting out a whistle. "Such soft flesh. So young. So smooth."

She clenched every part of her body she could, staring up at the ceiling. Tears pricked her eyes. She wanted to reach down and pull up her sweatpants, but she was afraid that doing so would encourage him to grab her again.

He surveyed her for a moment, his eyes roaming over her body. She stared upwards, blinking, trying not to remember her father, the way he would stare at her over the breakfast table like she was a piece of cattle being sized up for the market.

He grabbed her pants. She gasped. He tugged them back up. He grabbed her t-shirt and eased that down over her belly, his fingertips brushing her flesh. She clamped her mouth shut, afraid she might be sick.

"Good," he said. He looked over his shoulder toward the door. "Officer! She can go now."

CHAPTER THIRTY-SEVEN

THE JUDGE'S CHAMBERS TOOK THE FORM OF A SMALL office with high windows, the hum of traffic making its way up from the street outside. Diplomas and family photos lined the walls, as well as one of the judge with the Governor of Texas.

Judge Haynes eased herself into a high-backed chair behind the glass-topped desk. The three attorneys stood opposite. Kate was in the middle. Becca Lloyd, the Assistant DA, eyed her. She looked amused by this turn of events. On Kate's right hand side, Grace's state-appointed attorney shifted from foot to foot.

"So," said the judge. "I need an explanation."

"It's perfectly simple, ma'am," said Kate.

'Enough of the ma'aming, alright?"

"Sorry your Honor. Like I say, it's very simple. I'm taking over the case from my colleague here."

Judge Haynes turned to the defense attorney. "And Mr Singh, what are your views on this?"

He looked at Kate. She looked back into his eyes, trying to reassure him. Did he know who she was? A senior partner at one of the most prestigious criminal law firms in the city. The kind of firm that normally represented CEOs accused of embezzlement, wealthy husbands who'd beaten their wives, or well-to-do drink-drivers.

Did he understand that she could help Grace? That she had more experience than he, and access to more resources? Or would professional jealousy win out?

"Before my colleague responds," she said. "I'd just like to outline what our roles will be. I'll be lead counsel on this case, and Mr Singh here will be acting as co-counsel."

His eyes widened. Maybe he thought she was offering him a job at her firm; she hoped not. Either way, he wasn't losing the case. Not completely.

He turned to the judge. "My colleague is correct," he said. He had a high-pitched voice that caught on the *correct*. He cleared his throat. "She and I will be working together on the case." He gave Kate a look that said *you better not be making this up*. Kate offered him a smile in response.

Becca was sweating next to Kate; the heating was on high in here, and in the courtroom. Judge Haynes had bird-like features and was thin as a flamingo; she was well-known for feeling the cold.

"They can't just change it like this." She took a step forward. "Not without informing opposing counsel in advance."

The judge waved a hand in dismissal. "They shouldn't," she agreed. "But that doesn't mean they *can't*." She eyed Kate. Kate held her gaze, hoping the many years of good behavior in this woman's courtroom would hold her in good stead. She believed in respecting the judges, not challenging them unless absolutely necessary and then allowing the evidence to make the challenge instead of her own words.

Some of her colleagues thought it made her a toady; she thought it helped her win cases.

"Thank you," Kate said. "If you don't mind, we'd like to request a recess to confer. I need to check where my colleague has got to with his initial statement."

"Very well. It's lunchtime, and we haven't broken yet. You get an hour."

Kate smiled. Justice Haynes barely ate, and was hated by lawyers for limiting breaks. Kate knew to fill up on a hearty breakfast when she had a day in this judge's courtroom ahead of her.

"Thank you. We're grateful for your understanding."

"Yeah. Now get out of my chambers."

The three lawyers shuffled out, Becca last out of the door. Kate watched to make sure she didn't duck back inside for a private word with the judge.

Outside in the hallway, Matthew turned to her. "What the hell is this all about?" he hissed.

Kate cocked her head in Becca's direction. "Let's get coffee," she told him. "Somewhere away from here."

He screwed up his nose but followed her out of the building, lugging a massive and cheap-looking legal case; she'd need to see inside that.

She took him to a diner two blocks away, one that didn't get too much legal traffic. They ordered omelets and took a booth at the back.

"So I know who you are," he said as they sat down. "But you've probably never heard of me. Matthew Singh, public defender."

"Pleased to meet you." She shook his hand.

"I still don't get it. Why you barged into my case. It's hard to believe that White, Petersik and Abad is suddenly taking an interest in women like Grace Williams."

She leaned in. "Do you know where I've been the last two months?"

"No idea. Enlighten me."

She swigged her coffee. It was bitter. "Carswell."

"Carswell? That's a medical prison. Some sort of research trip, or something?"

"I was an inmate."

"Why?"

"You want to know, you look it up. But the important thing is I met Grace Williams there. And I know she's innocent."

"Of course she's innocent. The poor woman had a miscarriage."

"She claims she had a miscarriage."

"I have two doctors who'll back her up." His tone was grim.

"And I'm sure Becca has three who'll disagree with them. Including Grace's own obstetrician."

"What?"

"She didn't tell you?"

He slumped back, looking smaller. "No." He eyed her. "How did you know?"

"I made it my business to find out."

"She told you."

"I wish. She wouldn't talk to me."

The waitress arrived with their omelets: tomato and zucchini for Kate, and three cheese for Matthew. They waited until she was gone. Kate picked at her omelet, knowing this was the best food she'd get for a while.

"So why the hell do you want to help her if she wouldn't talk to you?" he asked.

"Because she needs the best possible representation. And I can help with that."

"Your firm is happy with it?"

She took a mouthful of her omelet. It was good, just off runny in the middle. She tried to remember when she'd last eaten zucchini.

"My firm has nothing to do with it. They let me go."

"They what?"

She placed her fork on the plate. "Keep your voice down, please. I just got out of jail, and they didn't want me around anymore. So I'm at a loose end, and I want to help. I hope you're OK with that."

"As long as you keep me on the case, I'm more than OK with that. I've followed your career. I know your record."

She allowed herself a smile. "Thanks. So, we're a team then?"

"As far as I'm concerned. But there's one problem."

"Yes?" She thought of Becca, the way she'd looked at Kate as they left the judge's chambers.

"Grace. She needs to sign you. You sure she will?"

CHAPTER THIRTY-EIGHT

"I TOLD YOU I DIDN'T NEED YOUR PITY."

Grace and Kate were in a small office along the hall from the courtroom. Grace was no longer wearing her jumpsuit, or the irons they'd put her in. Matthew, her lawyer, was outside, waiting for Kate to summon him.

"I know that, Grace. But do you want to miss your kids growing up?"

"It's none of your damn business."

"I've seen a photo. They're gorgeous. Especially Sissy. You must miss them."

Grace bristled. "Don't you go pulling on my heartstrings with talking about my kids like that. This isn't about my kids."

"But it is. Your kids are the key to this. We need a jury that'll be sympathetic to you as a woman, and a mother. We need a set of folks who don't want to make you miss out on their childhood."

Grace could feel heat rising in her chest. "I don't like being pushed around like some kind of toy."

Kate leaned against the wall. She was wearing a blue

suit that looked expensive and a pale gray shirt. She smelled of musk and wore subtle makeup, the kind that makes a woman look healthy instead of made-up. Grace knew she looked dreadful herself, despite the jeans and t-shirt they'd found to replace the orange jumpsuit.

"Look," Kate said. "The system pushes people like you around. It pushed me around too. That's why I want to help you."

"I already have a lawyer."

"Matthew's a good guy." Kate's eyes went to the door. "But he's young. He hasn't defended a case like this before."

"And you have?"

"Not exactly like this, no."

"So what the hell use are you to me?"

"Let me continue, please. I haven't defended a case like this before, because there hasn't been a case like this before. Not in Texas, anyway. And since the Supreme Court pushed abortion back to the state legislatures, that's what matters."

"So what makes you so uniquely qualified to defend me, then?"

Kate took a step forward. Grace stepped back, hitting the wall. This room was too small; she felt claustrophobic.

"I know how hard it's been for you, Grace. We shared a cell, remember. I know what you went through."

Grace frowned. "You don't know what you're talking about."

"I've defended plenty of criminal cases. Including some that weren't exactly run of the mill. I'm good at thinking on my feet. I can sniff out precedent a mile off. Look at me, Grace."

Grace forced herself to look the other woman up and

down, aware that she was sneering but unable to wipe the expression off her face.

"Look at my suit. This haircut. I earn a lot of money, Grace. You said it yourself, on the day I left Carswell. I do that because I win cases. And I'm going to win yours."

"You only just got out of jail yourself."

"That makes me even more motivated."

"You just want to get back at them, for what they did to you. You don't care about me."

Kate slumped into a chair. "Yes, you're right. I'm angry. I'm angry that I had to have an illegal abortion when I found out I was pregnant by a man who'd been hitting on my teenage daughter. I'm angry that the doctor I got those pills from is still in jail. I'm angry that they took my eggs, twice. There could be kids out there with my DNA in nine months, and I'd never know about it. How do you expect that to make me feel?"

Grace straightened, her gaze still on Kate. "See. This is about you. It's all about you."

"I'm not going to lie to you. Maybe I wouldn't have taken your case if all that hadn't happened to me. Maybe I would. I have no way of knowing. But the reality is it gives me fire. It makes me motivated. I want to get you acquitted more than any other lawyer could."

"Matthew wants to get me off. He's been with me from the start. He's seen Linton, he knows my family."

"That's another thing. We have to not talk about Linton being in jail."

"Why not? He's a victim just as much as you think you are."

"The jury won't care about that. All they'll see is a woman from a family that gets itself into trouble with the law. We don't mention Linton."

"He's my husband. He's the father of my kids. He's innocent."

"I know all that, but we need to focus on your case here. Not his."

Grace shook her head. She didn't like this.

"Please, Grace. Give me a chance. I won't be charging you. This is pro bono. And I'll keep Matthew on the team. He knows your case, he's an asset."

"I don't like the way you talk about people. Like they're just things."

"Sorry. The legal system rubs off on you. Matthew's a good guy. He can help. And so can I."

"You keep him on?"

"Of course."

"And if I change my mind, you'll drop out and let him take over again. Or maybe you'll let me find my own lawyer."

"You don't have the money."

"How the hell do you know how much money I do and don't have? I had a good job, before all this happened."

"At the school. I know. I also know they cut your hours."

Grace felt her body sag. "You've been checking up on me."

"If you let me represent you, I'll check up on everything and everyone I need to. I'll do all I can to win for you, and let you go home to those beautiful children of yours."

"Don't bring my kids into it."

"We have to. They were witnesses. Boo calling the ambulance. Sissy going to your neighbor. And the jury will be more sympathetic to a woman who has three children who love her."

"You're not putting them in front of all those people."

"It'll be by video. We'll do it in advance. You can see the recording before anyone else does."

Grace stepped away from the wall. This woman seemed to know what she was doing. She still didn't like her, but then, she didn't have to like her. She just had to believe she could win.

And she certainly wanted to. You could tell that just by looking at the way her nostrils flared when she talked about the case.

"OK," she said. "But it had better be good, or I'm firing your ass."

CHAPTER THIRTY-NINE

Maya had been back home for almost a week now. Her disciplinary hearing had been put back when the prison had heard about the attack.

But she didn't want it put back; she wanted it over with. To defend herself. To get her life back.

She'd had enough of watching daytime TV, of reading and pottering around her cramped kitchen. Today was a cool morning, the kind she used to relish when she had a job and a reason to get up in the morning. She leaned against the window, looking out at the growing dawn, considering her options.

Her coffee was cold. With a heavy sigh, she poured it down the drain and switched on the filter machine for a second cup. She'd been drinking too much of the stuff; the old twitch in her cheek from excess caffeine was coming back. But if she didn't, she would find herself drifting off to sleep in the afternoons, sitting on her couch in front of the TV or dropping the book she was reading on the floor, the thud waking her with a start.

The coffee maker clicked and she grabbed another cup.

This time it was hot and sharp. She drank it down, ignoring the fact that she was scalding her lips. She leaned against the window again and watched the street come to life.

A figure was making its way along the sidewalk, a woman wearing an expensive-looking coat, struggling on the uneven surface in heels. Maya watched as the woman almost slipped on the sidewalk in front of her neighbor's house, which had the roots of an oak tree bursting through it.

The woman stepped over the roots then stopped to look up at Maya's building. Maya ducked behind the curtain.

After a moment or two, she shifted back into position, expecting to see the woman a few doors further along. But she'd disappeared.

Maya shifted closer into the window and leaned her forehead on the glass. The woman was on the step, the top of her brown-haired head right beneath Maya. She wondered who would be getting a visit from such a well-dressed woman at this time of the morning.

Her intercom buzzed and she flinched, spilling coffee on her sweater. She cursed and licked her thumb, which had also caught a splash. Brushing at her sweater, she crossed to the intercom.

"Hello?"

"Hi. Is that Doctor Maya Henderson?"

Maya felt something shift inside her. "Yes," she replied in a small voice. This couldn't be good.

"My name is Kate Mitchell. I was a patient of yours."

Maya pictured the woman making her way along the sidewalk. She didn't recall ever seeing anyone as upscale as that in the STD clinic, and as for the jail...

"I think you've made a mistake. I work at Carswell FMC."

"I know. I was an inmate until a week ago. Kate Mitchell."

Maya's hand went to her face. "Oh my God. Of course. I'm sorry, Kate. Come on up."

She buzzed the outer door open and hurried to her own front door. She looked frightful; coffee-stained sweater, jeans that hadn't been washed in over a fortnight and had interesting stains of their own and a pair of tiger slippers that her ex had bought her back when the two of them were on speaking terms. She should have known, as soon as she unwrapped that parcel.

Kate was hurrying up the stairs, bringing a cold draft with her. She smiled as she saw Maya in the doorway.

"I hope you don't mind me disturbing you this early in the morning," she said. "But it's important."

"Are you OK? Have you had complications?"

Kate paused in her tracks, frowning. It was as if she'd forgotten she'd been in prison, or why. Looking at the way she was dressed, Maya guessed that was easy to do.

"No," said Kate. "It's about Grace."

Maya felt herself pale. Grace had been recovering when she'd last seen her, but the woman was fragile despite her tough outer shell, and desperately in need of support.

"She's had complications?"

"No. No, not that. It's her case. Her trial."

"Oh." Maya felt stupid; she'd forgotten that Grace's trial was due. Her job was to focus on the women's health, to make sure they were well enough to provide the reproductive material the state demanded of them. To her mind, her job was to make that process as bearable as possible. She tried not to think about the legal process.

"How can I help?"

"I'm not sure. But I think they'll listen to you. Can I come in?"

"Of course you can."

Maya hadn't realized she was blocking the door. She pulled back and let Kate slide past her, taking in her scent of soap and expensive perfume. Kate looked briefly around the apartment and took a seat at the kitchen table. She placed her briefcase—leather, pristine—in front of her and started pulling out files and notebooks. She looked up at Maya, her face expectant.

"I'm sorry," she said. "You didn't offer me a seat."

"It's fine." Maya tried to ignore the dirty dishes and the heap of unwashed towels in the corner. She spotted a used teabag on the floor and pushed it toward the trashcan with her foot. "Let me get you a coffee."

"That would be fabulous, thank you." Kate sounded different out here from how she had in prison. The tables were turned; Kate was in charge. Maya admired her ease at putting her life back together after release.

Kate drank half her coffee down in one gulp. "I needed that, thank you. I'll get straight to it. I'm representing Grace in her trial, which is due to recommence tomorrow. I need all the help I can get, and I think you can help us."

CHAPTER FORTY

Kate couldn't host case meetings in the halfway house. Maya was worried her apartment might be watched by her employers. The only reliable space was Matthew's.

Sandra had filed a motion with the family court, and a custody hearing was scheduled in three weeks, on December 23rd. Even if she won, the chances of celebrating a normal family Christmas with Sasha were slim.

She'd tried to call Sasha, but her daughter's cellphone was switched off and Julian was refusing to hand over the landline. She knew she had the right to speak to her daughter, but the holding of a right and the exercising of it were two very different things. If she tried to force it, or to go around him, the authorities would view that harshly. His lawyer was already painting her as some kind of scarlet woman, unfit to raise a healthy teen.

She shook off her jacket in Matthew's hallway and hung it on the hook at the bottom of the stairs. Upstairs, she could hear voices: a woman and a child, giggling. She looked at Matthew.

"I didn't know you had a family."

He shrugged. "Just one girl. Zoe. She's nine." His eyes danced as he glanced up the stairs. Kate heard a shriek and then loud shushing.

"Is it OK us being here?"

"It's fine. Lola—that's my wife—she's used to it."

"Thanks."

"This way."

She followed him through to a formal dining room, a heavy mahogany table at the center surrounded by upholstered chairs. Papers were strewn across the table and piled high on the sideboard at the other end of the room.

"I guess you don't get to eat in here too often."

He laughed. "No."

Maya had already arrived. Kate went to her, hand outstretched. "Thanks for coming. I know it's a risk for you."

"On that subject. Can you subpoena me?"

Kate nodded; Maya had been doing her homework. "I might be able to, if we have grounds. That way, you have no choice but to testify."

Maya sat down. "What kind of grounds would you need?"

"Well, I'd need to request a record of your meetings with Grace, to start. I need to have reason to believe she might have given you information that's pertinent to her case. Or that your examinations can prove that she had a miscarriage and not an abortion."

"I didn't see her until a week after it happened. There was evidence of scarring, but it could have happened when she was examined in the ER. God knows how many people touched her or what they did."

"Surely there are records."

"In a busy ER, things can get lost. They had no idea the

case might be suspicious, not until the cops turned up the next day."

"You know that?"

"I'm assuming that from what Grace told me."

"What *did* she tell you?"

"Not much, to be honest."

"Wait," said Matthew. "What about her state of mind? Can we show that the miscarriage made her depressed?"

"An abortion might just as well have the same impact," said Maya. "And she's learned that her baby was going to be born severely sick. She had no end of reasons to be depressed."

"What about the kids?" said Matthew. "Have they said anything about what happened?"

"Beats me," said Kate. "I thought you'd know about that."

Matthew blushed. "Sorry. I'll see if I can talk to them tomorrow."

"Go easy on them," said Kate. "We don't know how much they know, or how they've been affected by it all. And we'll have to get the permission of the court to speak to them at all. Judge Haynes has slapped an order on them."

"Damn," said Matthew. "That better apply to the prosecution too."

"It does," said Kate. "But they'll have sources. The kids have been taken into care. I'm sure Becca will find a way of getting at whoever runs the facility they're in."

"What about me?" asked Maya.

"Sorry?" said Kate and Matthew in unison.

"I'm a doctor. There'll be doctors there. Maybe I know someone."

Kate shook her head. "You're on thin enough ice as it is. No, leave this one with us. I want to do this by the book."

"Very well."

"Shall I get coffee?" asked Matthew. "Looks like we'll be here a while."

"Please," said Kate. "Black, strong," said Maya.

Matthew grinned, the grin of a man who wasn't used to being part of a team. He slipped out of the door and Kate and Maya settled in to weigh up their options.

CHAPTER FORTY-ONE

THE JAIL UNDER THE COURTHOUSE WAS DAMP AND chilly. Grace's cell had one high window through which she could see a moody gray sky and the occasional bird. Way up in the distance, a plane flew over, a faint white line following it across the sky. She wondered where it was going, and whether she would see the inside of an airplane again.

She sat on the thin bench that lined one wall of the cell, her arms clutched around her belly. She still had the occasional twinge, her uterus shrinking after so many months carrying the poor doomed child. She knew that her body produced oxytocin after childbirth, that it helped the uterus get back to normal, and provoked twinges when it was released. They called it the 'love drug', because it came when women looked at their babies with love.

She would have loved that little boy. However short his young life had been, and however hard, she would have given him all the love she could. Seeing her other kids going through the pain of losing a sibling would be gut-wrenching, but she would have done it. Somehow. She'd briefly considered ending things more quickly for this poor baby, it had been one of the hundreds of thoughts in her head when she'd asked the doctor about her options. And she knew that in the old days, she would have been offered the alternative of an abortion. But a part of her was glad now that she hadn't had to make that decision. Which would she prioritize; sparing her living children the pain of seeing their little brother die, or putting the poor innocent child to death?

The child had made its own decision, or else God had. The miscarriage had been a mercy, although it still made her eyes fill with tears every time she thought of it. The baby hadn't been planned; Linton had drunk a few too many beers one night and in his haste to get her into the bedroom, they'd forgotten to fetch her diaphragm. She'd assumed she was too old to catch anyway. And then Linton had been arrested just a month after her twelve-week scan, and things had become suddenly much, much harder.

She wondered if Linton was in a cell like this one now. She still didn't know if he'd been given a trial date yet. Just another brother accused of a low-level violent crime he didn't commit. An elderly white woman had picked out his photograph, a photograph they only had on file because he'd been caught shoplifting when he was in his twenties. And now he was abandoned in the system somewhere.

She'd watched in the courtroom four days ago as Kate, that do-gooding white woman from the prison, had barged in and taken over control. The young man who'd been appointed to defend her, Matthew, seemed the good kind. He was doing the best he could. But she knew he was inexperienced, and that his best maybe wasn't good enough.

She hated to admit it, but she needed Kate's help. Kate

was a good lawyer, she could tell. You didn't get to dress like that unless you'd won a few cases.

The door to her cell squealed open. She sat upright, refusing to let them see her beaten. A guard stared in at her, a well-built black woman who looked a few years younger than Grace and refused to meet Grace's eye. Instead, her gaze roamed across the cell, finally alighting on the window above Grace's head.

"Time to go," she grunted.

Grace stood up, her head high. "Where are you taking me?"

The guard looked her in the eye for the first time. She looked like she didn't know whether to be sympathetic, or mistrustful. "Upstairs."

Upstairs could mean anything; Grace had no idea how this worked. The first time, it had been for a meeting with Matthew. The second had been for her trial, so abruptly interrupted. Maybe they were about to continue.

"Is my trial starting up again?"

"Lady, you got a lotta questions."

"I deserve to be told where you're taking me."

She heard movement behind the guard; another guard, this one a slim white man. "What's she want?" he asked his colleague.

The young guard turned. "Wants us to tell her where she's being taken."

The man grinned at Grace. "She does, does she?"

"Yeah."

"Shall we tell her?"

Grace watched the two of them in silence. She knew better than to interrupt when the guards decided to toy with you, that having a right wasn't the same as being allowed to use that right. What was she going to do if they refused to tell her? It was her word against theirs.

"Well," sneered the male guard. "We could be taking you home."

Grace kept her face still, refusing to react to the idea of being released.

"We could be taking you to see your kids."

She pulled in a breath; what did they know about her kids?

"Or we could be taking you to your trial."

She stared ahead, focusing on a damp patch on the wall.

"Which one do you think it is, inmate?" the man said. His colleague looked down, not meeting Grace's eye.

"My trial," Grace replied.

"Sorry? Can't hear ya."

"Your colleague told me you were taking me upstairs. That means my trial."

"Bingo!" He laughed. "Put these on her, Roberts."

Roberts took the shackles from him and started to truss Grace up. Grace held her arms out to the side as the woman fastened the belt around her waist, blinking back tears. Then she put her arms down in front as they attached her wrists to the belt. Finally, her feet were shackled. She was turned three times for them to check her.

"She's going nowhere," said the man. "Well, not unless we want her to."

The woman gave her a tiny smile, one that might have been an apology. Or might not. "Come on," she said. Her cheeks were ruddy, and her hair was done in a modern style.

Grace shuffled forward. The shackles weren't as tight as last time and she had enough freedom of movement in her arms to be able to swing them ever so slightly as she walked. She gave the female guard a *thank you* look. The guard nodded in return.

"Move, bitch!" the man snapped. She started to move before he had the opportunity to shove her.

CHAPTER FORTY-TWO

KATE CROSSED AND UNCROSSED HER LEGS AS MATTHEW rose to restart his opening statement. They had a new jury now; the only thing unchanged was the judge. Judge Haynes watched Matthew with her sharp blue eyes. Kate respected this woman; she hadn't always won cases in her courtroom, but she'd been treated fairly, and her clients had been given a genuine hearing.

In the witness stand was a woman Kate recognized from the deposition video Matthew had taken before she'd come on the case. Veronica Hillard was Grace's neighbor, a thin woman who looked as if she could do with a few more meals and a lot more sleep. She wore a pale green skirt suit that almost disappeared against the green of the leather witness chair, and a nervous expression that Kate hoped the jury wouldn't mistake for fear.

"Mrs Hillard," said Matthew, "would you tell us about your relationship with Grace Williams and her family please?"

Good, thought Kate. They'd agreed to mention Grace's

kids as often as possible. They'd gained agreement from the judge that her husband's arrest couldn't be mentioned in court, as it had no bearing on the loss of Grace's baby. But mentioning Charlie, Boo and Sissy would help their case. She'd met the three of them herself that morning; an aunt had brought them to the court, and Matthew had told her to take them away again. They'd already given evidence on video; they wouldn't be called on again, thank God.

"Grace and me are neighbors. I live in the house next to hers."

"How long have you known Grace?"

"Three years. Since I moved in. She was there five years before that, since Sissy was born."

"Can you tell us who Sissy is?"

"Sorry. Sissy is her girl. She also has Charlie and Boo, two boys."

"Do you see much of the children?"

"I sit for them when Grace has to work nights."

Kate frowned. She didn't want Grace depicted as a neglectful mother. She looked across at the jury. Four of them were black now, and eight female. But three of the women looked like they came from the sort of neighborhood she did. Having to get your neighbor to mind your kids because you were holding down two jobs to make ends meet would be alien to them.

"What work does Grace do?" Matthew asked.

"She's a middle school teacher, at Johnston High. And sometimes she does cleaning work in the evenings, and tuition. Since they cut her hours at the school."

"When was this?"

"Eight months ago. Budget cuts, they said. Told Grace she was last in, so first to get her hours cut."

"How long has she been a teacher?"

"I'm not sure about that, but since before I've known her."

"But you say she was last in."

"Oh. Sorry. Yeah, she worked at another school before that, not sure which one. For ten or so years, I think. You'd have to ask her." Veronica looked toward Grace, sitting next to Kate. Grace nodded back at her friend.

"Thanks, Mrs Hillard. I'd like to ask you about the evening of fifteenth September, if that's alright."

"Of course it is. That's what I'm here for."

Some of the jury flashed each other smiles. Kate grimaced but kept her head straight.

"Thank you, Mrs Hillard."

Kate stared at Matthew's back. *Don't reinforce it. She's here to tell the truth, not to do as she's told.*

"My pleasure."

One of the jury—a white man in the back row—snorted. Kate looked from him quickly back to the witness, who seemed oblivious.

"Can you tell me what happened on the night of September fifteen please."

"Of course. I was at home on my own, watching TV. Err... *Grey's Anatomy*, I think it was. There was a loud knock on the door. I remember it making me jump out of my skin."

"Who was at the door?" Matthew asked.

"It was little Sissy. She looked scared."

"Scared?"

"Yeah, like she did sometimes when she got in trouble at home. Sissy had a mischievous streak a mile wide, sometimes her daddy would have to punish her."

There was muttering among the jury. Judge Haynes cleared her throat and it died down.

"What did she say to you?" Matthew asked.

Kate rolled her eyes. At the table opposite, Becca Lloyd was rocking back in her chair, smiling. Matthew seemed oblivious. *Turn it around*, Kate thought, staring at his back. She wished she'd paid for him to get a new suit.

"She said her mom was sick."

"And what did you do?"

"I left my house—locking the door, of course—and followed her. Oh no, I went back inside first, to make sure I didn't leave the stove on. I didn't want my dinner burnin', see."

"What did you find, when you arrived at Grace's house? Were her other children there?"

"Charlie was nowhere to be seen. Boo was standing next to his mom, crying his eyes out. I had no idea what to think. I thought maybe Linton had been convicted or something."

More muttering. Matthew turned to flash Kate a look. Kate lifted herself up in her chair, then forced herself to sit again. She looked across at the jury; three of the jurors in the front row were whispering amongst themselves, leaning across. Next to her, Grace was holding herself very still, her eyes on the witness, her cheeks flushed. Kate could see her chest rising and falling.

Judge Haynes looked annoyed. "Please strike the witness's last statement off the record," she said. "Ladies and gentlemen of the jury, please ignore what she just said."

"Why?" one of the jurors asked; a middle-aged woman in a purple dress.

The judge gave her a look. "Because it isn't relevant to

this case. Mr Singh, carry on. Or do you need me to call a recess?"

"No," he said. "I'll continue."

Kate stood up. "Actually, ma'am, we would like to request a five-minute break. I need to confer with my colleague."

Matthew looked around at her, his eyes hard. She ignored him.

"Five minutes, please?"

"Very well. But no longer."

The judge slid out of her chair and the jury were led outside. They looked at Grace as they left, puzzled looks on their faces. Grace kept her head straight and her eyes ahead. She looked calm, as if she'd been prepared. They had to work on her warmth, thought Kate.

"What the hell was that?" Matthew hissed. Becca turned and looked at him, a lopsided smile on her face. Kate glared at her.

"I think I need to ask you that," whispered Kate. "How come you didn't warn her not to mention Linton?"

"I did," he pleaded. "She just didn't listen."

"Now the jury knows that Grace has a husband in prison. They'll be thinking that she didn't want to raise a fourth child on her own. That she comes from a family of criminals. We're screwed."

"We have more witnesses," he said.

"She was one of our best."

"Sorry."

Grace was being led away by a guard. She looked back at her lawyers, her eyes large and sad. Kate felt like she'd betrayed her. Taking on the case like this had made her feel like some sort of savior swooping in to fix things. Now they were even worse.

"I'm taking over," she said.

"You can't."

"After the break. I'll tell the judge I'll carry on with questioning."

"Kate, you can't," Matthew repeated.

"I'm going to damn well try."

CHAPTER FORTY-THREE

"Now, you aren't going to cause me trouble again today, are you?"

Cindee bit down on her lower lip, refusing to meet the doctor's eye. He was leaning back in his chair opposite her. At least he hadn't dragged it round next to her this time.

"Well? Answer me."

"No," she muttered.

"Good. You understand now that if you give me trouble, I will have you restrained. I need to examine you and your baby and it would be easier for both of us if you just let me do it."

"Yes."

"Good." He smiled and stood up. "I'm glad we understand each other."

She looked back at the door, wondering if the guard was still standing outside. Would someone come, if she screamed? Would she dare to scream anyway? Would she be able to?

"Get on the couch," he said.

She dragged herself to the couch and sat on it. He gave her a look of annoyance.

"Lie down. You know the score."

She felt a cold fist grip her inside. Her stomach churning, she pulled up her t-shirt and lay down, her feet dangling over the side.

"Pants too," he snapped.

She pulled the waistband of her pants down just a little, almost to the bottom of her bump. Her pubic hair was growing back; she hadn't been able to get hold of a razor since she'd arrived here.

He sighed. "Come on, Cindee. I need access to the full length of your bump, so I can measure the fundal height."

She pulled her waistband down a little further, allowing herself to hope that she was being paranoid. Maybe all he would do was measure the baby's height, listen to its heartbeat, and send her on her way.

Even so, she'd rather have another doctor doing it.

"That's better. Now lie still."

She held her breath and lay as still as she could, hoping that if she cooperated, this might be over sooner. He placed his fingertips on the center of her stomach and pushed.

"Ow."

"I told you to be quiet."

He twisted his fingers around, pushing and prodding in a way that gouged at her flesh. Every time he moved his hand, she gasped. But she managed not to cry out.

Suddenly his fingers left her skin. She tensed, waiting for what came next.

He leaned back, surveying her.

"You really are a little slut, aren't you Cindee?"

She blinked up at the ceiling, unable to speak.

"Who's the father of this brat, huh? Some kid you fucked when you were bunking off school, no doubt."

She bit her bottom lip, feeling the metallic tang of blood in her mouth. She blinked back the fizz of tears.

He leaned over her. "Not going to tell me?"

She swallowed. Her throat was dry and her chest heavy.

"How's the baby?" she croaked. "Your examination, is it OK?"

He barked a laugh. "As if you care. You wanted it dead."

More tears fell down the side of her face and into her hair. She stifled a sob, thinking of Suze taking her to the clinic. Suze had found her in the bathroom after she'd taken some pills she'd gotten from the pharmacy. Pills she'd been told would end the pregnancy. Pills that hadn't done that, but had nearly killed her.

Then she thought of the commotion outside Suze's door the other day. How come her mom hadn't been summoned? Surely now she would get a visit.

"What did you do with my sister?" she asked. "Where is she?"

"How should I know?" He placed his hand on her stomach again. The fingers were warm this time. She tensed, wondering if the baby could feel his sharp fingertips through her skin.

She closed her eyes then opened them again. The darkness behind her eyelids just took her back to her bedroom. At least here she wasn't with *him*.

Not that this was any better.

He flattened his hand on her stomach. "You want this thing dead, don't you Cindee?"

"No."

"You sure? You aren't lying to me?"

"No."

"You're making no sense. No you aren't sure, or no you aren't lying to me. It has to be one or the other."

"No I'm not lying. No I don't want it dead."

"Hmm. I could help, you know."

She blinked; the tears were drying now, overcome by confusion. He leaned his head over hers, his face directly above her. "You don't want to know how?"

She shook her head. She had no idea if she wanted this child; but she didn't want him touching her. Or hurting it.

"Stupid girl. It would be better for everyone, including the poor goddamn child."

She pursed her lips; they were dry.

He stared down at her for a moment, moving his hand across her stomach all the while. She held his gaze, struggling against the need to squeeze her eyes shut. At last it was too much and she closed her eyes, clamping out the sight of his face.

"Open your eyes, Cindee."

She blinked them open.

"Good. This won't take long."

His hand moved down her stomach. She sucked in her breath, trying to pull inside herself. He wormed his hand down her belly, twisting and rubbing as he went. He was checking the baby, she told herself. That was all.

At last he reached the bottom of her bump. He cupped his hand and squeezed, making her gasp.

"That hurt?" he said.

She nodded. "A little."

"Hmmm." He squeezed harder. Then she felt the fabric of her pants move downwards; he was sliding them down her thighs. She sucked in breath. She felt faint.

"Stop," she whispered. He ignored her, instead giving

her belly a final squeeze then worming his fingers down between her legs. She whimpered.

She opened her eyes. Above her was the damp-stained ceiling. His face had gone. He was somewhere outside her range of vision, looking at her, watching his own hands violating her. She opened her mouth but nothing came out. She lifted her arms by her sides but something heavy was on them, holding her down.

She opened her mouth again, forcing out air. A rasping sigh came from her lips.

He had his fingers inside her now, three or four of them, she couldn't tell. His breath was heavy, and he grunted.

Visions flashed in front of her eyes, images of her father weighing her down in her bed at night. The room went light then dark then suddenly light again as she saw her darkened bedroom, followed by the pale ceiling of the examination room and then her bedroom again. She felt something rise from her stomach.

"You bitch!"

He pulled away from her, brushing at his suit. She stared at him, watching him come into and out of focus. Her face felt warm and her hands were covered in something wet.

She realized she was vomiting. She leaned over the side of the bed and puked onto the floor, long and loud. He shrank back, his feet shifting on the tiles to get away from her.

"You're disgusting,," he spat.

Good. Better to be disgusting than to be desirable. She let her stomach empty itself onto the floor, remembering the thin oatmeal she'd had at breakfast. On the way out it was sharp and acrid.

At last her stomach was empty. She dry-heaved a few

times then pushed herself up, her arms stiff. He was staring at her.

There was banging at the door behind him.

"Everything OK in there? You alright doc?"

He turned to the door, his face red. "I'm fine! The patient is just unwell, is all. Don't come in."

She stared at the door, wide-eyed. *Come in*, she urged. *Come in, now.*

He slapped at her thighs, causing her to groan in pain.

"Make yourself decent," he hissed. "You look a state."

She glared at him through eyes crusted with tears and God knew what else. She reached blindly for her pants and yanked them up as she slid down from the bed.

"I need to go," she muttered.

"Go. Get out of my sight."

She ran to the door and pounded on it.

CHAPTER FORTY-FOUR

GRACE WAS LED BACK INTO THE COURTROOM. HER lawyers had stopped arguing between themselves and were sitting side by side, their faces hard. She looked at Kate, trying to figure out the woman's motives. She had her own life to rebuild after prison, her own family to focus on. And now she was failing to fix Grace's situation.

The guard gestured toward the seat next to Matthew, and Grace sat down. Once the jury had filed in, Kate stood up. She approached the judge.

"Your Honor, I would like to apologize for the disruption a short while ago. I will be continuing with the questioning of our first witness."

"You have that little faith in Mr Singh?" The judge's eyebrow was arched.

"It's not that. But I have prepared for the second part of this questioning. I would like to continue with this witness."

The woman in the tight floral dress on the table opposite, the one who'd tried to make out that Grace was some kind of monster, stood up. Rebecca Lloyd, Assistant DA. Grace watched her, feeling her stomach clench.

"This is not only extremely unprofessional of the defense, but also unfair on the witness," she said.

The judge sighed. "It's not all that unusual to switch lawyers in the middle of cross examination. Not all that common either, but I don't see any reason why not."

"I do," replied Rebecca.

The judge turned to a man standing by the door at the front of the courtroom. "Please don't bring the jury back in just yet." She turned back to Rebecca. "Go on."

"Until just two weeks ago, Kate Mitchell was herself a prisoner at Carswell FMC. She's currently living in a halfway house in Austin."

"That doesn't preclude her from working as an attorney, or from representing clients," said the judge. "Your crime didn't relate to your position as an attorney, did it Ms Mitchell?"

"No, your Honor."

"You didn't embezzle money, or commit fraud?"

"No, your Honor."

"Well, then."

"It's not as simple as that," said the other lawyer.

The judge gave her a look that said *spit it out*.

"Ms Mitchell is no longer a partner with White, Petersik and Abad. They fired her."

The judge leaned back in her chair. Grace felt the hairs on the pack of her neck prickle.

"You didn't tell us that." She raised a pen to her mouth then put it down. "So who are you with now, Ms Mitchell?"

"I'm establishing my own firm, Ma'am."

"You've established your own legal practice?"

"I'm in the process of doing that, yes."

The judge raised a hand. "Wait a minute. You say you

haven't completed the procedure of registering your firm to practice law in the state of Texas."

"The registrar's office is currently processing the final paperwork."

Next to Grace, Matthew fidgeted in his seat.

"Then in that case you need to leave," the judge said.

"Ma'am..."

"No. You finish your paperwork, and you can come back. But until then, your colleague Mr Singh is sole counsel for the defendant."

Matthew stood up; he approached the bench. "May I request a recess of two days so that my colleague can complete the necessary paperwork and we can mount a proper defense?"

"No, you may not." The judge glared at him. "I've had enough disruption in this case. I say we get to it. Ms Mitchell, you must leave now, before I have to call for security. Mr Singh, I suggest you finish questioning your witness."

Matthew and Kate gave each other startled looks. Grace stared at Kate, horrified that after all the other woman had promised her, she was about to let her down. She could only hope that Vee would realize what she had said wrong, and put things right. That the other witnesses would repair the damage.

The jury were returning to the room, looking around as if they could piece together what had been happening in their absence. Becca returned to her table, her eyes dancing.

Kate was next to Grace now, rooting through her files and stuffing them into a briefcase. She looked at Grace.

"I'm sorry, " she said.

CHAPTER FORTY-FIVE

KATE SLUMPED ONTO THE COURTHOUSE STEPS, HER legs unable to carry her any further. She dropped her bags on the ground and plunged her hands into her lap.

She leaned over, burying her face in her skirt. It smelled of an unfamiliar washing powder: Sandra's.

Packing her bags and leaving the courtroom had been hell. Grace had looked angry and disappointed, a look that reminded Kate of her childhood, the many times her mother had kicked off at her.

Grace had needed her help and she had failed her. She'd talked Maya into joining their campaign, and now she'd abandoned Maya and Matthew to do this alone.

And Matthew was struggling. His cross-examination of Vee had been sloppy and given her too much opportunity to veer away from their preparation. And the jury, having seen Grace's legal team fall apart, would be mistrustful of the remaining team member. She wondered what reason the judge would give them for the change, if any. Either way, they would be speculating; they might even think Kate had left because she believed her client to be guilty.

She felt air stir beside her as two men hurried down the steps, parting around her and not pausing their conversation as they did so. They were gossiping about a lawyer whose name she recognized, a partner at a rival firm. She thought about Claude, the way he had looked at her when he'd fired her. About Tom Abad, and the fact that he hadn't returned any of the twenty-three calls she'd made to him since.

She had no choice but to drop this. Maybe it was a blessing: she could focus on Sasha now, on getting her daughter back. A hearing was due in just ten days, time enough for this trial to be over and for Sandra to prepare her. She knew what she was going to say, anyway. But Sandra had told her that she needed to allow for the judge; whether they had a pro-choice judge or a pro-life one would be everything. If she had a pro-life one, she was screwed.

She stood and looked up at the courthouse. She'd spent the last twenty years of her life in this place. Now it was barred to her.

She needed a drink. And a friend. Dragging her heels, she made her way down the steps, pulling out her cellphone to call Sandra.

CHAPTER FORTY-SIX

"You look rough."

Cindee shrugged. Dora, her cell mate, meant well. But there was no way she was telling anyone what had happened with the doctor. What was the point? Who would the prison authorities believe?

"You can tell me about it, you know."

Cindee gave Dora a thin smile. Dora scared her; she was huge, about thirty tattoos just on her arms, and a confidence that made Cindee wonder if she'd been here before. Cindee hated that the women didn't talk about what had got them sent here; it meant she didn't know who she should be scared of.

"I'm fine." She turned over in her bunk and faced the wall, folding her arms across her chest.

"You don't look fine."

Cindee listened to Dora moving around the space. She was expecting a visitor this afternoon, her husband. He was six-foot-four and built like a wall. Dora described him as a pussycat but Cindee wasn't so sure. Dora would be making herself look nice right now; styling her hair, putting on makeup. Cindee never failed to be amazed at how much makeup some of the women wore on visiting day.

Dora had said nothing about the fact that Cindee never got visitors, but she knew the other women talked about it. A girl of her age should have some family come visit, unless they were all dead or locked up themselves. Cindee knew there was a rumor that she came from an infamous crime family. It would have been laughable, if the reason for it hadn't been so depressing.

Surely with Suze sick, their mom would come visit? If she was angry with Cindee, maybe she wouldn't be so angry with Suze. Or maybe she was even more angry with Suze; most of Suze's life had been characterized by loud fights with their parents. But Suze was lying in the hospital somewhere, unable to breathe without artificial assistance. She'd taken Vicodin, a pain reliever.

"Is it that new doctor? Did he hurt you?"

Dora had stopped moving and was standing next to the bed. Cindee could hear her breathing, the heavy tones of a smoker.

"I heard about him. He does stuff to young girls like you."

Cindee curled her legs beneath her. Her stomach hurt from the pressure he'd put on it, and she ached inside from his angry fingers pulling at her. She couldn't say anything though. If she did, she had no way of knowing how she would hold in the fact that this baby was not just her father's grandchild, but his own child too.

"Leave me," she whispered.

"I'm going to kill that man," Dora breathed.

Which man? Then Cindee remembered Dora had been talking about the doctor. She turned round.

"You can't say anything. He'll hurt me. He'll tell them I asked for it."

Dora shook her head. "So he *did* hurt you."

"I didn't say that." Cindee closed her eyes. This was too much for her. It was a like a dam behind her eyes, behind her lips. Just waiting to explode.

"Please," she said. "I don't want to get into trouble. For my sister."

"Your sister is away from him now. This don't affect her."

Cindee shook her head, powerless.

"That man needs stopping," Dora said, her voice harsh. "You wait here."

She hurried out of the cell. Cindee listened to her footsteps receding down the hall, her mind numb.

CHAPTER FORTY-SEVEN

Maya watched Matthew approach her in the
witness stand. She chewed her bottom lip, wishing it was
Kate doing this.

She could hear the clamor of voices outside; protesters,
on both sides of the argument. She wondered by which
route Grace had been brought into the building.

Either way, looking at Grace, she could tell her former
patient was able to hear the protesters. Grace would assume
they were all against her, believing her a murderer. Maya
had watched a preacher on last night's news, claiming that
Grace's unborn child had been failed by his family and by
the state. In his eyes, the child was ruthlessly slaughtered by
a selfish, uncaring mother who was more interested in her
own convenience than the life of a child.

Kate had fought to win anonymity for Grace, but the
press had got hold of her sister Sylvia and from that moment
on it had been a free-for-all, with names all over the internet, the children being photographed on their way to school,
and Grace's name dragged through the dirt. Even if she won

her freedom, she was going to have a rough time once she got out of here.

"Doctor Henderson." Matthew gave her a hesitant smile. "You were Grace's doctor at Carswell Federal Medical Center, is that right?"

She nodded and glanced at the jury.

"Can you explain what kind of medical center Carswell is, for the jury?"

Most of them were looking at her, some at Grace. "It's a federal prison, for women who have medical conditions or are undergoing medical procedures."

"Thank you. And you were the defendant's doctor there."

"Yes."

"Can you tell me when you first examined her?"

"Our first meeting was on October seventeenth. That wasn't an examination, but an initial consultation. She then came back to me on the twenty fourth, for an examination."

"What kind of examination was that?"

"It was an internal exam, designed to check the health of the patient's reproductive organs."

"Is this a routine procedure for a prison doctor?"

"Not generally, no. But I specialize in obstetrics and gynecology, so it's the kind of thing I do all the time."

"Does Carswell keep you on staff, or do you just come in for the occasional case?"

"I'm on staff. My main job is to process the women who've been convicted under the abortion laws."

"What exactly are you required to carry out with these women?"

"I extract their genetic material."

"I'm sorry, doctor. I'm not quite sure I follow. What does that mean?"

Maya swallowed. They'd agreed to discuss this, even though Grace hadn't been subject to it yet. She would be if convicted. "I harvest their eggs."

Muttering from the jury; the judge looked up and it stopped.

"This is the statutory sentence for a woman who obtains an illegal abortion, is that right?"

"Yes. They're subject to a prison term during which their eggs are harvested."

"And do you know what happens to these eggs?"

"Not exactly, no. I assume they're used to help infertile couples."

Matthew smiled at her. "Thank you. Did you perform this procedure on Grace Williams?"

"No. She had too recently been pregnant. She wasn't ovulating yet."

"But if she had been?"

"Prisoners on remand are sometimes subject to harvesting, yes."

"Even though they have not yet been convicted?"

"Yes."

"Can you tell me what procedure you did carry out on the defendant?"

Maya allowed herself another glance at the jury. Two of the men were looking downwards, blushes creeping across their skin. The women were all looking at Grace.

"I examined the health of Grace's reproductive organs."

"And what were the results of your examination?"

"The patient—Grace—had minor abrasions to her vagina."

They'd gone through this. She was to stick to the facts. Only speculate if he asked her too. So far, so good.

"What would normally cause these kind of abrasions?"

"They were consistent with emergency treatment for a miscarriage. A speculum would have been used to open up her vagina, so she could be examined."

"So these abrasions, or scratches, would have occurred at the hospital after Grace was admitted?"

"Most likely."

"Thank you. Did you have an opportunity to examine the defendant again?"

"No." Maya's throat tightened. "She was allocated another doctor."

"No further questions."

Maya shot him a grateful smile. He'd done well. He'd used the language they'd agreed, and so had she. But now she had the Assistant DA to face.

She licked her lips and pulled her back straight as she waited for Becca Lloyd to approach. Kate had warned her about this woman; she moved slow, but her mind was sharp.

Becca ambled up to the bench as if she had all the time in the world. Maya watched her, then remembered she was supposed to glance at the jury from time to time, as well as at Grace. She let her eyes roam over the jurors. Most of them were watching Becca's journey to the front of the courtroom. Two of them were watching Maya. She gave them a quick but small smile and let her eyes glide on until they rested on Grace, who was staring at her, her cheeks flushed and her chest heaving.

Maya frowned. What had happened so far in the courtroom?

"Ms Henderson," said Becca.

"Dr Henderson."

Becca didn't reply. Instead she turned to look at the jury, probably rolling her eyes. Maya forced herself not to react.

Becca turned back to her, a wide but insincere smile running across her face. "Thank you for taking the time to be with us today."

Maya nodded. This wasn't a question, so she didn't need to answer.

Becca waited a moment, then continued. "Please can you remind the court when you last saw the defendant."

"Eighteenth of October."

"October eighteenth. Five weeks ago."

"Yes."

"Can you tell me the reason why you haven't seen her more recently? I imagine a woman whose body has been through what hers has would need follow-up care."

"I haven't been at work."

Becca turned to the jury. She took a couple of steps toward them, her eyes passing over them. A couple of them looked at her and smiled nervously.

She looked over her shoulder at Maya. "Is it true that you haven't been in work because you were suspended?"

Kate had told her to be ready for this. "That is true. It doesn't affect the fact that I was Grace's doctor when she was first admitted and conducted a thorough ex—"

"Can you tell us why you were suspended?"

A pause. The jury's eyes were on Maya now.

"That's confidential."

Becca turned to her. "Confidential? Why?" Her voice had the lilt of someone who genuinely wanted an answer to their question. Maya knew as well as Becca did that she already knew the answer.

"Because I'm awaiting a hearing."

"What kind of hearing, *Doctor* Henderson?"

"A disciplinary hearing."

"Can you tell us what you were disciplined for?"

"I haven't been disciplined. That only happens if the hearing finds against me."

"Alright." Becca was looking at the jury again. Beyond her, Matthew was sinking in his chair, his eyes on the prosecutor. "So what happens if this hearing does find against you?"

"If that were to happen, I would lose my job."

"Your job?"

"Yes. I would be dismissed from the Texas Department of Corrections."

Becca turned back to her. She was smiling, a genuine smile this time.

"Doctor Henderson, is it correct that you were suspended because you provided the defendant with information that you were specifically told not to?"

Maya held herself very still. "Like I said, I can't talk about the details of the hearing. Not while it's ongoing."

"Hmm." Becca tapped her teeth with her fingernails. Maya wanted to grab those shiny pink fingers and make her stop.

"So. You can't talk about whether or not you were disciplined because you showed favoritism to the defendant here."

Maya said nothing. She watched Matthew, waiting for him to interrupt.

"What else *can* you talk about?" Becca asked.

Maya starred at her. That was one hell of an open question, for a lawyer in court. "I can talk about my patient's health when I examined her. I can talk about the fact that in my professional opinion Grace Williams had injuries consistent with a miscarriage and subsequent treatment in hospital. They were not consistent with a late-term abortion. Especially not a self-inflicted one, which would have been significantly more violent."

"Your professional opinion."

Maya looked at Matthew again. *Help me out here.* But he was watching Becca, as entranced as the rest of the room. Maya wanted to jump up and down and demand that she be asked a question.

"Do you think we should value your professional opinion?" Becca asked, in a casual tone.

Maya looked at Matthew. He was watching the jury, his face pale. Then he spotted her staring at him and leapt to his feet.

"Objection!"

Judge Haynes turned to him. "I was wondering when you might say something. On what grounds?"

"The prosecution is goading the witness."

"Goading? I don't think. so. You may continue, Ms Lloyd."

Becca smiled. "Ms Henderson, please answer the question."

"I do," she said. "I've been practicing medicine for twenty-two years, eighteen of those specializing in Ob-Gyn. I have lots of experience of treating women who've had miscarriages, and women who've had abortions."

"But if this disciplinary process goes against you, you will no longer be a medical professional, is that correct?"

"Not necessarily."

Becca cocked her head. "Come, now. Is it not true that if you are fired by the State of Texas Board of Corrections, you would most likely also be struck off the General Medical Register? And that you would no longer be able to practice medicine?"

"It's unlikely that—"

"Please answer my question. Is it possible that you will be struck off, Ms Henderson?"

Maya swallowed. She gave Matthew a look. He spotted her staring at him and leapt to his feet.

"Objection! The prosecution is speculating."

"Hmmm. You're shooting very close to the wind, Miss Lloyd. Try another question."

Becca nodded. "Dr Henderson. You have been called here as an expert witness because, as you reminded me, you are a practicing medical doctor. Is that correct?"

"Yes." Maya twisted her toes in her tight shoes, wishing she hadn't agreed to this.

"And if you should be struck off because of this current investigation, that would no longer be the case, am I right?'

Maya wanted to punch her. She had a sudden image of those men at the bus stop, the ones who believed it was OK to sexually assault women just because they were there. The cops still hadn't caught them; she wasn't sure they were even trying.

"Dr Henderson, I need an answer. Is there a possibility that because of actions you took with regard to the defendant, you could be struck off and no longer allowed to practice medicine?"

"A slim possibility."

"But a possibility, nonetheless?"

"Yes."

"Thank you. No further questions."

CHAPTER FORTY-EIGHT

KATE WALKED PAST THE DOOR TO SANDRA'S APARTMENT block for the third time. She'd been released from the halfway house but was unable to face the prospect of packing up her stuff at home. She was pursuing a claim against the landlord, but Kate wasn't the type to become a squatter.

Sandra was on the phone to Sasha; as the last person Sasha had been living with before she'd gone with Julian, she had been allowed a phone call with Kate's daughter. The family court judge presiding over the case had decided it was a fair compromise. But he hadn't allowed Kate to speak to her daughter, and she'd been ordered to leave the apartment while the call was taking place.

She looked up at the windows of Sandra's apartment on the third floor; a light shone from the kitchen. She imagined her friend in there, talking to her daughter. Sasha had grown up with Sandra around, but they'd had little contact once Sasha hit the teenage years. What would they talk about?

She pulled her jacket around her and turned the corner,

picking up pace. As she turned the next corner, her cell-phone beeped. *All clear. She's OK. Come back.*

The apartment door was already open when Kate arrived.

"How was she?"

"She was quiet. Not sad quiet, but sorta shy."

"How much does she know about what's going on?"

"She knows about the hearing. She knows that the two of you are fighting for custody. I don't think he's keeping it from her, if that's what you think. Come on in, I've made you a coffee."

Kate sat at the kitchen table and wrapped her hands around the mug. "Did you tell her I miss her? That I can't wait to see her again?"

"Of course I did." Sandra put a hand on top of Kate's. "Don't worry, honey. We'll get her back. He's barely spoken to her in the last two years. His case is flimsy."

"He hasn't been to prison for killing her unborn brother or sister."

"Don't talk like that. You did what you had to do. How would it have been for Sasha, if you'd had Robert's child? After everything you've told me about that man, you did the only thing you could."

Sandra was right. If Robert had been behaving inappro-priately toward Sasha, or worse, then bringing his child into their family would only make things worse. And if Julian ever got wind of it, he would use it against her.

"How was she?"

"You already asked me that. She was fine. She wants to see you."

"I can't do anything about that."

"She *will* see you, soon. You aren't asking for sole

custody. He is. You're being way more reasonable, and the judge will appreciate that."

"I don't like the idea of him having her on vacations."

"It's the only bargaining chip we have. If you didn't show some willingness to compromise, then all I have to work with is a mother who's had an abortion, been to prison, and wants her daughter all to herself. This shows that you're interested in her wellbeing, not just your own."

"Unlike him."

"Exactly."

"Do you really think we could win?"

"Yes. Judge Shapiro is a conservative, but if there's one thing he can't stand, it's kids not having access to both parents. Julian's lawyer is from out of town and won't know that. I think that's our trump card."

"I sure hope so." Kate swigged down the last of her coffee and stood to fetch another cup. She held a hand out toward Sandra's cup, her eyebrows raised.

"No thanks," said Sandra. "Early start."

"I was hoping to discuss the Williams case with you before going to bed."

"I trawled through the library at work, but I couldn't find any useful case law. The legislation is just too fresh. Your case is the first real test of this part of it."

"It's not my case. Not anymore."

"Sorry. I couldn't find anything on defense lawyers just out of jail, either. At least, nothing less than a hundred years old and so archaic it's barely relevant."

"Right."

"Sorry, Kate. I'm not an expert on this stuff. Can't you think of anything?"

"Not without access to a law library. I can't even get at

an online one; my access was revoked when I was convicted, and they haven't gotten around to giving it back yet."

"Then you're going to have to trust this Matthew guy."

"Yeah." Kate dragged a hand through her hair.

She poured her coffee and sat back down, heavily. She felt more tired than she had since she'd been studying for the bar exam. Matthew had called her on her cellphone while she'd been out pacing the streets. To tell her things hadn't gone so well with Maya Henderson.

They didn't have enough witnesses, was part of the problem. No one at the hospital was prepared to testify, and what friends and neighbors they could find weren't much use. They'd been relying on Maya, and Becca had torn her apart.

Grace needed a solid witness. Someone who could tell the jury just how badly she'd been affected by the miscarriage. Someone who knew she hadn't killed her own child. Someone who would stand up to Becca Lloyd and not let her get the better of them.

She put her coffee down, almost spilling it.

"You OK?" Sandra was checking emails on her laptop. She looked across the screen at Kate, her eyebrows raised.

"I'm fine."

"Fine?"

"Yes. Fine."

"Why the sudden change?"

"Because I've figured it out."

"Figured out what?"

"How I can get myself back onto Grace Williams's case."

CHAPTER FORTY-NINE

CINDEE WAS WOKEN BY SHOUTING FROM THE HALLWAY. She lay still, hoping it would go away. In the bunk above her there was no familiar sag; Dora was already up.

She turned onto her side to face the room, expecting Dora to be there, getting dressed. It was rare that Cindee woke after Dora. She was used to early mornings at home, having to leave the house at 6.30am to catch the school bus.

The room was empty.

She pulled the thin blanket tighter around herself, longing to sink back into sleep. But if Dora was gone, it meant breakfast would be soon, if she hadn't already missed it. And immediately before breakfast was inspection. The COs skipped it some days, relying on the unpredictability to confuse the inmates. But on the morning after visiting, they never missed inspection. They claimed it was to check no contraband had worked its way into the prison during visiting hours. But the women were strip-searched after their visits, subjected to the indignity of squatting and coughing in case they'd hidden anything inside their bodies.

If anything had got through all that, it would have been safely hidden by now.

No, the post-visiting inspection was a way of reminding prisoners that they belonged here now, and that they were subject to the will of the COs.

Cindee heaved herself out of bed. She was already dressed; she'd adopted the habit of changing into tomorrow's clothes every night, so that she could be ready if she was woken by an inspection. All she had to do was make her bed, and that was hard enough. If the blanket wasn't folded under the mattress exactly right, it would be dragged off the bed and the inmate would be ordered to make the bed again and again until it was perfect.

Hurriedly, she made her bed then stood back to check it. It looked good enough to her eyes, but who could say if a grouchy CO would deem otherwise. She checked the bunk above; Dora's bed was neat too, just like her own. The cell was tidy, all of their personal belongings stashed safely away in the cupboard at the end of the bed. Dora had the top two shelves, Cindee the bottom one, because she was new.

The shouting intensified. Cindee pulled on the prison-issue black boots that made her slender feet ache. She stopped just before the door, not sure if she wanted to see out.

Eventually, curiosity overcame her. She leaned her head around the door and peered along the hallway, ready to withdraw quickly if she needed to.

The hallway was empty. At this time of day, there were normally women moving around the block; heading for breakfast, getting to their jobs. Or guards, doing their rounds.

She stepped out, wondering where everyone was. The shouting was coming from the other end of the hall, around a corner. As she headed for it, a woman barreled out of a cell and slammed into her.

"Watch out, kid!"

"Sorry." Cindee offered up a shrug of apology then hung back as the woman shoved her aside and ran towards the source of the commotion. Emboldened, Cindee followed.

She rounded the corner to see a thick crowd of women in the middle of the hallway. They were crowding in on each other, shouting, chanting and clapping. She heard cries of *get him* and *dirty bastard*.

The crowd shifted as two COs dove into it from the opposite direction. Cindee shrank back as women scattered around her, pushing past her in their haste to get away. A fight may be great entertainment, but no one wanted to be caught in the midst of it.

A few women remained at the center of the crowd, bent over a figure on the ground. They were laying on blows, kicking something, screaming. It was like they had lost their minds. Two of them were young. As young as Cindee. Another was older; she looked like she could be the mother of one of the girls. They had the same white-blonde hair and thin lips. And another was Dora.

Cindee shrank back even further. If her cellmate was in the center of this, she could be blamed. Especially if the victim was who she thought it might be.

She heard a man cry out, his voice high. A woman screamed *pervert*. The crowd shifted and swayed, and two women tumbled out. The man yelled again. "Fucking bitches!" There was a slamming sound and his voice was cut off.

Four more guards arrived, waving batons at the women who'd pulled away. The women scattered, the hall emptying out. Cindee stared at Dora, unable to move.

The COs dragged the women up and away from each other, pulling them by the collar, the sleeve, the hair, whatever they could get their hands on. One of the women, the one who looked like the daughter, was thrown to the floor. A female CO put her knee on the girl's back while the girl writhed beneath her, screaming.

In the middle of it all, two more guards were huddled over Dr Abbott, who lay motionless on the floor. Cindee stared at him, hardly daring to breathe. She had no idea if he was alive or dead. At last he groaned and made the slightest movement of his arm. One of the guards bent down to mutter in his ear.

The doctor raised his head, grimacing in pain. One of his eyes was plastered shut by a layer of congealing blood. With the other, he looked around the space. His gaze landed on Cindee.

She shrank back, her heart pounding. If he singled her out, they would put her in solitary. She would never get probation. She was due to be released a month after the baby was born, in February.

She caught hold of her senses and turned. She sped around the corner as fast as her belly would let her and slid to the floor, her breath thin. She had to get up again, to keep running until she got to her cell. The other COs hadn't seen her; it was only his word. Although his word was way more powerful than hers.

She ran to her cell and landed on the bed with a thud. She considered whether it would be better to climb back under the covers, and risk being unprepared for inspection. That would give her an alibi, perhaps.

She lifted the blanket, keeping it as straight as she could, and slid under it. She turned away from the door, wishing she'd closed it, and stared at the breeze block wall a few inches away from her. nose.

She heard footsteps and pulled in her breath. Someone was at the door. It wouldn't be Dora. Dora would be in solitary by now.

"Adams."

She feigned waking up, dragging a fist across her face and yawning. She'd never make an actress. She turned onto her other side, then pretended to be shocked as she saw the CO in the doorway. She stumbled out of bed, almost tripping over the blanket.

"Why the hell is your bed unmade?"

"I overslept. I'm sorry."

"Hmpf." The guard was female, one of the women she'd seen restraining Dora. Had she seen Cindee? Could she know what Dr Abbott had been doing to the women?

"I didn't see it," she said. "Straighten it up before I return."

She turned and left the room. Cindee listened to her footsteps, her head light.

CHAPTER FIFTY

THE DOCTOR'S TESTIMONY HADN'T GONE WELL. Without Kate on the case, Grace knew she was going to jail for a long time. Matthew stumbled on with the defense, but he was way out of his depth.

They were questioning a guy called Doctor Cho, someone she'd never even met, Doctor Henderson's boss, no more relevant than a random stranger on the street.

The Assistant DA asked him a few questions about his career—psychiatry specialist, working in hospitals, moving to the prison system ten years ago, working his way up to management.

"Dr Cho," the prosecutor said. "I'd like to ask you about information that was sent to you by the hospital where the defendant was treated after she lost her baby."

The doctor was a slim Asian man with a thin smile and an outbreak of acne on his chin. He nodded. "We were sent the inmate's results by email just after she arrived with us. There was an internal exam, and blood tests."

"Can you tell the court the results of those tests?"

"The internal exam was inconclusive. I believe that in

the heat of the emergency situation, they didn't keep full records."

"Is that normal, Dr Cho?"

"In a busy ER, it's difficult to keep track of everything."

"But what *were* they able to tell you, doctor?"

"She was examined for evidence of a pessary being inserted into her vagina. Sometimes women use them to bring on an abortion. There was no evidence of that, so I asked one of my team to carry out our own examination."

"Doctor Maya Henderson performed that examination, is that right?"

"It is."

"And what did she find?"

"She found evidence of scarring to the vagina."

"What might that scarring have been caused by?"

"Dr Henderson believed it had been caused by the use of a speculum to open up the patient's vagina when she was admitted to the ER."

"And do you agree with this conclusion?"

"Scarring can also be consistent with the insertion of an instrument to bring about an abortion."

"What kind of instrument?"

"Anything sharp and thin, often metal, but sometimes plastic. Coat hangers are often used."

"Are you aware that the police found an unraveled coat hanger in the defendant's home?"

"I wasn't."

Matthew stood up. "Your honor, this isn't a question. We've already seen this evidence from the police, and we've learned that the coat hanger in question was being used by Grace's daughter for a craft project."

The Assistant DA put up her hand. "I apologize, your Honor. Let me move on to another question."

The judge nodded. She looked tired. Grace looked over at the jury; some of them were fidgeting and one had his head tilted back. It was past lunchtime.

"Dr Cho," the prosecutor continued, "I expect that Mr Singh will have colluded with Dr Henderson on this subject. He will challenge you on your assertion that the scarring could be consistent with an abortion. So before he does, please can you answer this: is there any reason for you to doubt the impartiality of Dr Henderson's conclusions?"

"There certainly is."

"Please can you tell us those reasons."

"Dr Henderson is currently undergoing investigation for falsifying patient test results. She destroyed a set of results and replaced them with a fake."

The prosecutor smiled. "Whose test results were these?"

Dr Cho looked at Grace. "They were Grace Williams's test results. Maya Henderson destroyed evidence that Ms Williams took an herbal tea known to bring on abortion."

The prosecutor looked shocked. The man on the jury who had been leaning back straightened himself up and looked at Grace. She stared at Matthew: *what's going on?*

"Dr Cho, please explain," said the prosecutor.

"The defendant had traces of raspberry leaf tea in her system. It's an herb known to cause contractions. Taken in a large enough dose, it can bring on an abortion."

"And do you think Dr Henderson concealed those results because she believed Grace Williams had used raspberry leaf tea to kill her baby?

"I do."

The prosecutor turned to Matthew and smiled. "No further questions."

Matthew was on his feet immediately.

"Dr Cho, I have just two questions for you. Well, three I guess."

Grace frowned at him. Was her attorney getting into his stride, or was he about to screw things up?

"My first question is this: according to those tests, how much raspberry leaf tea had Grace drunk?"

"I wouldn't know."

"Can you estimate?"

Dr Cho frowned. "If forced to, I would say three or four cups."

"So, the sort of quantity a person might have if they were simply drinking an herbal tea they believed to be innocuous?"

"Enough to cause an abortion."

"Really?" Matthew walked back toward Grace. He grabbed his briefcase and brought out a packet of tea. "Your Honor, I would like to admit this pack of tea into evidence. It is the same brand as Grace had in her kitchen. She had no idea of its effects."

"Your Honor, the defense is testifying."

"True. Mr Singh, tone it down."

"Sorry, your Honor. I would like to read the warning leaflet inside."

"Go on."

He opened the box and withdrew a slip of paper. "Warning: potential risk of miscarriage if taken by pregnant women. Do not consume this product during the first trimester of pregnancy." He paused and handed the box and its contents to the clerk. "Dr Cho, how many weeks pregnant was Grace when she miscarried?"

"Twenty-one weeks."

"Is that in the first trimester?"

"No."

"Do you really think that at twenty-one weeks of pregnancy, three or four cups of this tea could have brought on a miscarriage?"

"Well, given the state of health of the baby..."

"Do you really think this is what caused my clients' miscarriage?"

"I don't know, but..."

"Thank you. I promised you I had a second line of questioning. Can you remind the court of your specialty, Dr Cho?"

"I'm a psychiatrist."

"Thank you. Do you have experience of dealing with Post Traumatic Stress Disorder, generally referred to as PTSD?"

"I don't see what..."

"Dr Cho, I'd like to remind you that you are under oath. Have you treated PTSD patients in the past?"

"I have."

"And when those patients have flashbacks, in your experience, do they relive the events that caused their trauma, or do they make things up?"

"Flashbacks tend to include accurate renderings of events that caused the patient trauma in the past. But I still don't..."

"No further questions."

CHAPTER FIFTY-ONE

KATE SAT IN THE HALLWAY OUTSIDE THE COURTROOM, twisting her hands in her lap. Her palms were sweating but she felt cold.

The door opened. She shifted in her seat, but it was a man she didn't recognize, a journalist maybe, not the bailiff.

She sat back. The door opened again.

"Kate Mitchell."

She sprang up. "That's me."

The bailiff sniffed. He was a tall, gangly man with a large nose and a squint. "Come with me."

She allowed herself a smile as he turned to lead her into the courtroom.

Inside, the courtroom was full. Matthew turned as she entered and threw her an encouraging smile. He looked harassed; his hair messed up, his tie crooked. She'd helped him prepare for Brian Cho's testimony, and she knew it had gone well. But the exchange he would have gone through while she was in the hall outside would have been tough.

Across the aisle, Becca Lloyd was glaring at her. Kate

pushed down her smile; looking smug would do nothing to help Grace.

Grace was facing forward, sitting next to Matthew. Kate watched her as she passed, trying to gauge her mood. She was wearing the pink suit Kate had picked out for her. It suited her, made her look more feminine than the austere black thing she'd worn to her bail hearing. She was even wearing a small amount of makeup.

Kate walked to the witness stand, her heart rattling in her chest. The last time she'd done this had been her own case; she'd stood in the stand and pled guilty. She'd had nothing she could have used in support of a not guilty plea, no way of claiming she hadn't gone to the clinic that day in search of an illegal abortion. There were no extenuating circumstances, in Texas law.

She focused on her breathing during the swearing-in, running through the familiar words on auto pilot. She'd lost count of the number of times she'd witnessed this. At last she was asked to sit.

She shuffled in her chair. The jury's eyes were on her; she knew better than to stare back. Instead, she looked at Matthew, and then Grace. Meeting Grace's eye would emphasize the trust the two women had for each other, and the fact that Kate was telling the truth.

"Can you tell us what your relationship is with the defendant please?" Matthew asked.

"She and I were cell mates in Carswell Federal Medical Facility."

"When was this?"

"We met when she moved into my cell on November third. We shared a cell until November twentieth, when I was released."

"And can you tell us why you were in jail?"

She looked at the jury. "I caught my ex making advances on my teenage daughter. I ended the relationship, and then discovered I was pregnant. I had an abortion at seven weeks into the pregnancy and was sentenced to two months in jail for offenses under the Right to Life Act."

Only four of the jurors were still looking at her; two women, and two men. The others were looking at Matthew. She had a sudden panic. She'd agreed with Matthew that she would be brief, and candid. But maybe they now looked at her, a woman who'd let a potential abuser into her house and killed her unborn child, in the same way the state did.

She felt her mouth fill with saliva. She took a deep breath. *Focus.*

"What kind of relationship did you have with Grace?"

"We were on speaking terms, but not what you would call friendly."

"Did you talk about your respective crimes at all?"

"No. You don't do that, in prison. Everyone wants to know how long you have to serve, but no one asks what you did to find yourself there."

"So you didn't know that Grace had had a miscarriage, and been accused of performing an abortion on herself."

"I knew she'd done something under the reproductive legislation. That's all."

"How did you know that?"

"She was visiting the gynecologist, just like me."

"Doctor Maya Henderson."

"Yes."

"So you didn't become close. You weren't bosom buddies."

"No."

"So Grace didn't tell you about her miscarriage?"

"No. She talked about her kids though. Charlie, Boo

and Sissy. We showed each other photos. Her three, and my daughter."

"Your teenage daughter. The one you were trying to protect when you had your own abortion."

"Yes."

"Objection, your Honor." Becca Lloyd was on her feet. Kate was surprised she'd waited this long.

"On what grounds?" asked the judge.

"I'm wondering when the defense will get to the point. Does this witness have evidence, or is this just an excuse for her to work her way into this case after being kicked off it as defending counsel?"

"Fair point. Mr Singh, please move things along."

"Of course." Matthew feigned a look of disappointment. But this was good, this was what they had expected.

"Ms Mitchell. I'll get to the point," he said. Kate nodded. "Can you tell us what you know about the defendant's miscarriage?"

"Yes," Kate replied. "I know exactly what happened to her."

Two members of the jury turned to face her. She stared at Matthew, waiting.

"Go on," he said.

"She had flashbacks," Kate said. "At first they were in her sleep. But then it started when she was awake. I'm not sure she was entirely aware of what was happening."

"Can you explain what happened during these flashbacks?"

"It was like it was all happening again. She would describe the symptoms, just like she was having a miscarriage right there in our cell."

"Can you describe what these symptoms were, please."

"Objection! The defendant is not a medical doctor. She has no expertise." Becca was up again.

Judge Haynes frowned. "I'm intrigued. I'm going to let you continue, Mr Singh. But be careful."

"Yes, your Honor." He turned back to Kate. "Go on."

"First she would seem to experience pain. She'd collapse onto the floor of the cell. Then she would panic. She called out the names of her kids. Every time it was the same: Boo get on the phone to the ambulance, Sissy go next door to Vee. I'm not sure who Vee was."

"How did you know this was a miscarriage, and not the after-effects of an abortion?"

"Because of her reaction. She was shocked. Heartbroken. She would cry out, *no no no*. Then she would mutter, like her kids were in the room and she didn't want them to hear. The same words every time. 'No, baby. Not yet. God wants you to live. Momma wants you to live.'"

She looked at the jury. One of the women had pulled a tissue out of her bag and was wiping her eyes. All they had to do was plant reasonable doubt...

"Anything else?" Matthew asked.

"Yes. Afterward, she would cry silently in her bunk. She never let me near her, it was dreadful to watch. I don't think she knew who I was. She called me Sissy. One time, she apologized to me. She told me that my baby brother had decided not to join the family, that God was taking him."

She allowed herself a glance at Grace. Grace was staring at her, her eyes wet. Did she remember?

Matthew cleared his throat. There was murmuring from the public gallery. Another juror grabbed a tissue.

"What would you say to someone who suggested that these could be the ravings of a woman overcome by guilt at aborting this child, at deliberately ending its life?"

"She wanted that baby to live. She held her belly, gently like she didn't want to hurt the baby that was no longer there. She stroked it. She begged it not to leave her. There was no way she wanted that baby to die."

Kate felt her chest constrict. She thought about Robert, and the child she might have had with him. She thought about Sasha. She'd done the right thing. She had to hold her existing family together.

"Is there anything else that Grace did during these flashbacks, that you'd like to tell us about?" Matthew asked.

"That's all there is. I'm sorry I had to witness such sorrow. Such deep regret."

Matthew nodded. He gave her a tight smile. She turned to Becca Lloyd, who was advancing on her.

CHAPTER FIFTY-TWO

CINDEE WAITED.

It had been three days, and she knew it wouldn't be long before they found out that she'd told Dora about Dr Abbott.

Part of her was awestruck at the idea that the women had come to her defense. She had no way of knowing if he hadn't done the same thing to other women here, maybe to those two girls she'd seen kicking him.

They'd turned on him. They'd seen him for what he was. They'd done what they could to stop him, or at least to get their revenge.

She, by contrast, had just stood there and watched. Worse: she'd tried to hide. And now here she was, lying on her bunk. Hiding. Again. She'd spent her whole life hiding from men who wanted to hurt her. Maybe it was time to come out of the shadows.

She took a deep breath. The baby was quiet today, maybe as subdued by the attack as she was. She was due another exam tomorrow. She had no idea if Dr Abbott would do it, or if he was too badly hurt. She hadn't seen him around the prison since. Unlike the other doctor, that *call me Maya* woman, he liked to roam the halls, chatting to the women. Flirting. Some of the women liked it; desperate for a good-looking man to pay them attention, they played up to it. But for most of them, he was a creep. And for Cindee, he was a monster.

She shifted in the bunk, trying to get comfortable. The baby spent most of its time pressing on her bladder or groin now. She was having even more trouble sleeping than before. They'd moved her to another cell, a larger one for women with severe medical conditions. She was sharing with a woman who had terminal cancer, an emaciated old soul whose hair fell out in the sink and whose skin seemed to hang off her like leaves from a tree.

The baby woke up at last, kicking her hard in the groin. "Stop it," she muttered. She'd tried to summon up some tenderness for this creature, some sense of wanting the thing that was growing inside her. But every time she imagined its birth, she remembered how it had gotten there in the first place. Would it look like its father? Given that she did herself, there was a good chance.

Inmates weren't allowed to keep their babies; they normally went to family. But what family did she have? Her sister was in here somewhere, God only knew where. And their mom had shown no sign of interest. She figured this kid would find its way into the care system. If it was lucky, it would be adopted. Couples were always looking for healthy babies. And she had no reason to believe this would be anything but healthy.

She was hungry. There were some crackers in her nightstand, bought from commissary with money she'd earned in the workshop. She pushed herself up in the bed, swinging her feet around to the floor. It was cold.

"Oof." The baby was kicking again. This time it was like

the thing was pushing at her in all directions. Like it had stretched out its arms and legs and was trying to burst out by force. She put a hand on her stomach, muttering a prayer under her breath. Even if she would never see this child after birth, she wanted it to be born healthy. It deserved that much.

She stood and almost slipped in a puddle on the floor. She sat down again, breathing heavily. The squeezing had stopped; her belly had gone quiet. She leaned over as best she could and checked the puddle. It hadn't been there before. One of the women on cleaning duty had been in here just an hour ago, mopping the floor. A privilege of being a whale was that she didn't have to clean her own floor.

She bit her lip. That was her waters on the floor. They'd broken.

The baby wasn't due for six weeks.

"Help!" she cried. Her cellmate was out, sitting in a hospital somewhere tied up to her chemo. The women in the surrounding cells would be out working or exercising, or sitting on their bunks with their ears closed against the noise of the prison.

"Help!" she called out again. A face appeared in the doorway: a CO.

"What is it? I don't have all..."

The CO spotted the liquid on the floor. She leaned out and hollered down the hall.

"Adams is in labor. Get down here, quick!"

CHAPTER FIFTY-THREE

GRACE COULD BARELY BREATHE AS PEOPLE FILED BACK into the courtroom.

Matthew slid into the seat beside her, sweating. He gave her a nervous smile and placed his hands on the table. There was a small pile of files and books; he straightened them, arranging them so everything was at right angles. Grace wished she had something of her own to touch, to fidget with. Her hands felt empty. All she had was the sleeve of her horrible pink suit which she kept tugging at. She feared she'd be back in prison clothes by nightfall.

Becca Lloyd and her team were next in. They sat at the table across the aisle, not looking at Grace or Matthew. They muttered between themselves, speculating no doubt. She wondered what would happen to Becca if she lost, if her job would be on the line. *Tough.*

Then came the judge. She was an elegant-looking white woman in her sixties, with a frown that scared Grace. Was she always this stern, or was that a persona? Kate had told her not to let herself be intimidated by the judge or anyone here, but that was easy for her to say. Unlike Grace, she'd been doing this all her life.

At last the jury were ushered in. They took their seats in silence, one or two of them glancing in Grace's direction, their faces giving nothing away. She felt her heart tighten. Vee was in the crowd behind her somewhere, and her sister Sylvia. She and Sylvia had never got on—Sylv was shallow with bad taste in men—but her sister had come through for her this time. She'd been visiting Linton in jail, and had let Kate know that his trial was coming up in the new year. The thought of it filled Grace with both hope and terror.

She stared ahead, trying not to move. She wanted to stand up and run away, not stop until she'd battered down the gates to the kids' school and gathered them up in her arms. She badly needed to feel their skin against hers; there was nothing quite like the warm softness of your babies' cheeks against your own. Not that Charlie would appreciate being thought of as her baby.

She crossed and uncrossed her legs, irritated by the way the stupid skirt restricted her movement. Kate had insisted that it feminized her and made her look more human. Grace would have preferred a pair of slacks. But Kate knew best.

Except she didn't, did she? Grace had had no idea about those flashbacks in their prison cell, and certainly no idea that Kate had been listening in and making notes she would pull out later in front of all these strangers.

The jury was going to think she was a lunatic and a monster, and she would be going to prison for a long time. There would be dozens of kids walking around Texas with her DNA, and she would know nothing about who they were.

The judge stood. Everyone followed suit. Matthew gave her a nudge and she stood too.

She clasped her hands in front of her stomach, back to its normal size. They were damp.

It was time.

CHAPTER FIFTY-FOUR

CINDEE HEARD THE DOOR OPEN. SHE STAYED STILL IN the bed, facing the window. She should be relishing the fact that there was a window next to her. She should be out of bed, standing by it and taking in what little view there was.

"Cin?"

Cindee opened her eyes. It had grown fully light; when the nurse had taken away her uneaten food, it had been still half dark.

She felt a hand on her back. She flinched; no touching between inmates.

"Cin? It's me, Suze. They let me come see you."

She had a headache. This was a hallucination, a product of the fever they'd been treating with antibiotics. Her sister wasn't really here. Her sister had taken an overdose.

There was movement at the end of the bed. Suze walked around it and finally came into view, blocking the light from the narrow window.

"Cin, I'm so sorry." Suze lowered herself so she was kneeling in front of her sister's face. She'd lost weight and her roots were growing out. But there was enough purple; it was her.

"Suze?" Cindee whispered.

Suze smiled. "It's me, Cin. Here to look after you."

Cin frowned. "You told me you couldn't look after me. That note."

"I'm sorry. That wasn't me. Not really. That was some version of me, trying to protect myself."

"I thought you were dead."

"Me too."

"Did you do it deliberately?" Cindee felt heat rise to her cheeks.

"Try to kill myself?" Suze paused. "I don't know. I think so."

"Why? What did they do to you?"

"It wasn't a *they*. It was a *he*. A doctor. I told them I was pregnant and they put me in solitary."

Suze felt her eyes widen. "You weren't already? When you came here?"

Suze shook her head. "No. They caught me passing on details of the clinics. There was a network of them, I was telling girls that needed to know about it. They raided the house and found a stack of leaflets."

"But you said that Dad..."

"He did. But that wasn't what got me arrested."

"Was Mom there? When they raided?"

"She was horrified."

"Shit."

Suze laughed. "That's the first time I ever heard you swear."

"Sorry."

"Don't be. I think you've earned the right."

Cindee stared at her sister for a while. "They took the baby. His baby."

"I know. It's what they said they'd do to mine."

"Sorry."

"Don't be. Turns out it was a false alarm anyway. But it was enough to get Dr Abbott suspended."

Doctor Abbott. Cindee thought of his hand inside her, the press of his weight on her body. A heavy numbness overcame her. "Good," she muttered.

Suze leaned over the bed. She lifted herself up so she could spread her body over her sister's. She'd done this when they were little, protecting her from the bears they'd imagined were outside their bedroom window.

"Have you seen Mom at all?" Cindee asked.

"Just the once. She came to visit me two days ago. Only took her two weeks after they wrote to tell her I'd OD'd."

"What did she say?"

"Not much. But she's moved out."

Cindee sat up in bed. Suze slid off her and grabbed a chair.

"She left Dad?" Cindee breathed.

A nod. "She's suing him for the house. She wouldn't say anything about what he did to us. I think she's in denial. But it's a start."

"Not much of a start, with us in here."

"You don't have long, if you're lucky you'll spend it all in here. I think that's why they let me come see you."

Cindee grabbed her sister's hand. "I'm glad they did."

"Me too."

"Will you be OK? The overdose?"

Suze slumped in her seat. "They pumped my stomach, gave me a shitload of antibiotics, God knows why. They've got a shrink coming in and talking to me every day, not that I'm telling him a goddamn thing." She laughed.

"How long will you be here?"

A shrug. "I'm still on remand. Who knows?"

"Hell, Suze."

Suze gave her a playful slap. "Stop with the cussing, you. I'll think they've switched you for someone else."

Cindee allowed herself a smile. "I love you, Suze."

"I love you too."

"We'll get you out of here. We'll get you the best lawyer there is. You and me will find ourselves somewhere to live."

"That sounds good, Cin. It really does."

CHAPTER FIFTY-FIVE

THE CLERK HANDED JUSTICE HAYNES A SLIP OF PAPER. She read it, then folded it, placing it on the desk in front of her. Kate, sitting in the audience behind Grace and Matthew, watched the judge's face, her chest tight.

Grace, right in front of her, sat very still, her head erect. If found guilty, she would be facing a life sentence. A third trimester abortion counted as manslaughter in the state of Texas. She would be separated from her family for years. She would never see Charlie, Boo and Sissy grow up.

Sylvia was in a diner across the street with the three kids. Matthew had tried to dissuade her, saying it was safer to keep them in school, but the woman was insistent.

Kate took in a sharp breath as the judge surveyed the courtroom.

"Have you reached a verdict?"

"Yes, your Honor." The foreperson was a short woman with thick brown curls. She wore a necklace that caught the light, blinding Kate as she watched the woman's face for signs of emotion.

"Let us hear it."

"We find the defendant not guilty."

The courtroom erupted. Grace jumped up and folded Matthew in a hug. She was six inches shorter than him but at this moment she seemed twice his size. He looked at Kate over Grace's shoulder and gave her a wink. She smiled back, feeling tension drain out of her. Now this was over, her mind was suddenly full of Sasha.

Grace turned in Matthew's arms. She spotted Kate in the crowd and pushed through the gate behind her to run to her former cell mate. She grabbed Kate's hand.

"Thank you," she said. "I underestimated you."

Kate shook her head. "The most important thing is that you didn't do it. You were innocent, and the jury saw that."

Grace's eyes were wet. She nodded. "Where's Sylvia?"

"She's across the street, with your kids."

Grace shrieked. Matthew was behind her, dragging her back. "They haven't let you go yet," he said. "You have to be dismissed."

Grace laughed. She wrapped Matthew in a hug. "Thank you," she said. "Thank you."

CHAPTER FIFTY-SIX

Kate drew up outside her house.

Fatigue washed over her. She'd put in an eighty-hour week at her new firm and needed a good night's sleep. But not until she'd taken a long bath.

She locked the car and hurried to the front door. She brought her keys out of her purse then hesitated. She smiled and rang the doorbell.

"Mom."

Kate leaned forward and gave Sasha a quick hug, before her daughter had time to pull away. "Hey."

"Did you forget your key again?"

Kate shoved her key into the pocket of her coat. "Uh, yeah. Sorry."

"One of these days you're gonna get home and I won't be here. Then what will you do?"

"You're always here, sweetie."

"I'm serious, Mom." Sasha closed the door and followed her into the kitchen. "Next week I'll be at Dad's."

Kate almost stumbled. She knew Kate would be going

to her father's for two weeks from Sunday, but didn't like being reminded of it.

When Sasha was eighteen, she would be able to choose her own living arrangements. But for now, it was here in Austin in term time, and California in the vacations. Kate was going to miss her.

"You have a visitor," Sasha told her.

"Oh?"

"I took her into the snug. I made her a coffee, hope that's ok."

"Er, yes. I guess. Who is it?"

Kate felt cold at the thought of people coming here and hanging out with Sasha when she was at work. Sasha was having counseling. She hadn't said much about Robert except for making it very clear that he had only touched her the twice. Thank God.

"Said her name's Maya."

Kate relaxed and hurried into the snug. "Maya?"

Maya was sitting near the window, her fingers laced around a cup of coffee. She stood up and gave Kate a hug.

"Kate. You have a lovely daughter."

"Thank you. It's good to see you. How did the hearing go?"

"Well, Brian wanted me gone."

"Oh." Kate sat down next to Maya. The fatigue was growing; she didn't have the energy for more bad news.

"But he didn't have much say in the matter."

"Oh?"

"They had to take me back, seeing as their other gynecologist is under investigation."

"Why?"

"He was assaulting the patients."

Kate shrank back. "Grace?"

"Not Grace. She was too old. No, Dr Abbott liked them young."

Kate felt a shiver travel through her body. She looked toward the kitchen. Sasha was playing loud eighties pop and couldn't hear them.

"Dr Robert Abbott?"

"That's the one. They recruited him just before they put me on suspension."

Kate felt faint. "That's why I never saw him."

"You know him?"

Again Kate looked at the door to the kitchen. She shivered.

"I did. Not anymore." She turned to Maya. "Let's not talk about him. You got your job back?"

"I did. Thanks for your advice. It helped that I knew how to answer the questions."

"It's all I could do, after you helped with Grace."

"How's the new firm going?"

Kate smiled. "Good. I took on a new case today. Suzette Adams. Currently on remand at Carswell. I'll be representing her at trial."

"Does she have a sister?"

Kate shrugged. "No idea. I haven't met her yet."

Maya shook her head. "There wouldn't be two of them there."

The door opened and Sasha's head appeared. "Anyone want a cookie?"

"A cookie?" Kate stood up. "You sure you don't want to keep them all to yourself?"

"I think I can spare two."

Maya leaned back in her chair. Kate followed Sasha into the kitchen, her chest tight. "Did you hear any of our conversation, honey?"

Sasha rolled her eyes. "I know better than to listen in when you're lawyering, Mom."

～

Thanks for reading this book. You can read more about the characters in *Unborn* via the Rachel McLean website.

Go to rachelmclean.com/cindee to read Cindee's prequel story and find out just what she went through to find herself in Carswell.

GOOD GIRL - READ CINDEE'S PREQUEL STORY FOR FREE

Cindee is a good girl. Everyone tells her so.

Her mother, her pastor, her teachers. And *him*...

He says she's as good as gold.

Read for free at rachelmclean.com/cindee.

ACKNOWLEDGMENTS

A few people helped me write this book and make it a better read than it would otherwise have been.

My editor Dexter Petley did his usual excellent job of spotting the errors and correcting my sloppy prose.

My beta team gave feedback on an early draft and helped me hone the book and improve it for readers. Thanks to Eleanor Brend, Robin Diver, Heide Goody, Jane Edwards, Kirsty Handley, Hazel Ward and my dad Malcolm McLean, who has a hawklike eye for errors.

This book is dedicated to the women around the world who are denied the freedom to make decisions about their own bodies. The world may feel like it's going backwards right now, but we will overcome.

I hope you enjoyed reading *Unborn*. It's my seventh book and one I've been fermenting for many years.

I like to write thrillers that make you think - stories that get your brain ticking and your heart pounding.

You can find out more at rachelmclean.com.

Or read on for the opening chapters of *A House Divided*, my bestselling dystopian political thriller.

Happy reading!

Rachel McLean

A HOUSE DIVIDED

by Rachel McLean

Part 1 in the Division Bell trilogy

OCTOBER 2019. LONDON

HAYLEY PRICE WAS DEAD, AND JENNIFER SINCLAIR WAS going to get the blame.

Never mind that Hayley took her own life. Never mind that someone in Bronzefield Prison had provided her with the tool. And never mind that the prison staff had taken their eyes off a woman on suicide watch.

As far as the media was concerned, Hayley's death was the fault of Jennifer Sinclair, Prisons Minister.

Today Jennifer would be making a statement in the House of Commons, explaining why Hayley had been allowed to die. And it needed to be good. The prison governor's job was at stake – of course – but so was her own.

It was five am, and Jennifer was up early, taking advantage of the quiet of her London flat. Little disturbed her from outside: the milkman making his way along the street below, a couple of late night revellers ending yesterday instead of beginning today. Inside, all was quiet. Her husband Yusuf hadn't stirred when she'd slipped out of bed and her two sons were fast asleep in sleeping bags on the living room floor, staying in London for a special occasion.

She sat on the floor of the kitchen, the only unin-
habited room, and stared at the sheet of paper. Her
civil servants had insisted on drafting a full speech, but
she knew she'd do better with notes. Thinking on her
feet had got her this far; hopefully it wouldn't fail
her now.

She glanced at the oven clock. Not long before Hassan
would wake to realise it was his tenth birthday. She didn't
want him to find her sitting on the floor.

She pushed herself up, rubbing her cramped legs, and
crept towards the bedroom. It was a treat having the whole
family here - normally they'd be at home in her Birmingham
constituency - but the timing of this crisis was far from
ideal.

She reached the door to the bedroom and heard movement behind her.

"Mummy?"

She looked round. Hassan was sitting up, rubbing his
eyes. His older brother Samir was still snoring.

She pushed the speech from her mind. "Morning,
darling. Happy birthday."

His eyes widened and he let out a shriek. He threw off
the sleeping bag and jumped up, pushing past her to wake
his dad.

"Daddy! Wake up!" he cried. Jennifer followed him
into the bedroom.

Yusuf sat up in bed and feigned a yawn.

"Hello? Why would anyone want to get up this early on
a Wednesday?"

"Daddy!" Hassan repeated, and jumped on him.
Grunts came from beneath the duvet. Jennifer sat on the
end of the bed and gave Hassan a hug.

Yusuf leaned in and wrapped his arms round both of

them. "Anyone would think it was a special day," he groaned, pulling back and throwing Jennifer a wink.

Hassan shrieked. "Daddy! It's my birthday!"

Yusuf threw back the quilt, grabbing Hassan in one swift movement and tickling him. Hassan shrieked with delight.

Yusuf laughed. "Go and get your brother, Mr Early Waker."

Hassan nodded and sprang for the door, confident in the knowledge that when he returned, there would be presents.

Five minutes later he dragged Samir into the room.

"Alright, alright, I'm coming," Samir moaned, yawning.

"You can't sleep in on my birthday," Hassan replied.

Samir shrugged. Four years older than his brother, he was becoming skinny, gangly even. His skin was pale with fatigue and he had dark circles under his eyes. He would have been up late watching YouTube videos on his phone, Jennifer knew. He tried to hide it but the glow from beneath his duvet – or sleeping bag – was a dead giveaway.

"Hello, love," she said, reaching out towards him. "Come and sit with us while Hassan trashes the place."

She shifted into the middle of the bed, making room. Samir glanced at her then perched on the edge of the mattress. He pulled his sleeping bag around his shoulders.

Jennifer pushed aside the stab of rejection and shifted her attention to Hassan, who was scrabbling under the bed for presents. Samir dived onto his brother, pretending to grab the presents first. Hassan pushed him off.

"Come on Samir," said Yusuf. "It's Hassan's day."

Samir scowled and Hassan emerged from under the bed, his face flushed. He passed a present to his brother. "It's OK. He can help me."

Jennifer threw Yusuf a smile. That was just like Hassan, always wanting to share with his brother.

"Go on then," she laughed. "Get ripping." Yusuf lifted her hand to his lips and kissed her fingertips, his eyes fixed on her face. The boys ignored them, intent on tearing open wrapping paper. Yusuf squeezed her hand, then dropped it and joined in with the boys, pushing wrapping paper to the floor. Jennifer sat back and watched, smiling to herself. Seeing her boys enjoy moments she'd never had as a child felt like an accomplishment.

Then her eyes glazed over and she turned away, the boys' cries fading.

She couldn't stop thinking about that damn speech.

~

F our hours later, Jennifer stepped into St Stephens' lobby, the high, vaulted space between the Commons Chamber and the rest of the House of Commons. MPs hurried in from their offices and staff dashed between meetings, clutching sheafs of paper and mobile phones. Against this backdrop, reporters threw questions to passing ministers or else talked intently to camera. The noise was overwhelming. As Jennifer ducked past a TV crew, she overheard her name. The reporter – Gillian Wakefield, from the BBC – had her hand up to her ear, listening to her anchor in the studio. She was nodding, a smile playing on her lips. Jennifer paused to listen, stepping out of the reporter's eyeline.

The reporter dropped her hand and straightened up.

"Well, Mark," she said, "Nothing official of course, but several sources indicate that the minister's position could well be at stake."

Jennifer stiffened. She pinched her fingers together, grinding a fingernail into the ball of her thumb.

She started moving again, regretting that she'd stopped. She was happy to face down the cameras – relished it, even – but right now she didn't need to be distracted from her speech. Later, she would do all the interviews they wanted and prove to the world that she wasn't going anywhere. But for now... she needed to focus on surviving.

"Ms Sinclair!" cried a voice. "I wonder if I could have a quick—"

They'd spotted her.

"Sorry." Jennifer slipped between the other MPs and disappeared into the chamber.

As she reached the double doors she felt a hand on her shoulder. She willed the irritation from her face and turned round, ready to face down the reporter. But it was John Hunter, Home Secretary. Her boss.

"John. Thank goodness."

He raised an eyebrow.

"Nothing. Just..." She shook her head. "Press attention."

"Not surprising."

No, not surprising at all, she thought.

His grey eyes were cold. "We need to talk." He glanced around. "Not here."

"But I was just—"

He pulled her to one side, towards the Strangers' Gallery. They huddled next to the wall, their heads close together. Jennifer leaned on the wood panelling.

"This needs to be good," he said.

She nodded. "It will be. You know it will."

His normally ruddy cheeks were pale. "Michael's got his eye on you."

Michael Stuart was the Prime Minister. Jennifer didn't

know whether he would be present for her statement, but she knew he would be watching.

"Of course," she replied. "He should do."

John allowed himself a laugh. "Confident, are we?"

She pulled back her shoulders. "Yes. I won't let you down. You know that."

"Right then. Let's see what you've got, eh?" He placed a hand in the small of her back and guided her to the chamber. As she pushed the doors open, he whispered in her ear.

"Meet me for lunch, afterwards. Members' Dining Room."

She frowned. Normally they spoke in his office, or sometimes hers. Why the Members' Dining Room?

He slipped past and she watched him work his way between their colleagues, shaking hands and slapping shoulders. She wished she had his ease.

She shuffled along the front bench, taking her place next to her boss. She looked sideways at him; he was twisted round in his seat, laughing with two backbenchers behind them. She watched, trying to work out how he did it. How he performed so well in public.

The dining room. It's a public space, she realised.

If the Home Secretary was going to sack her, she wouldn't be able to make a fuss.

OCTOBER 2019. LONDON

JENNIFER SMOOTHED HER PALMS ON HER SKIRT AND stood up, taking a deep breath.

Across the Chamber, the Opposition bristled with contempt. Order papers waved in the air and voices rose to the vaulted ceiling. She focused on the dispatch box in front of her, trying to drown out the nagging voice inside her head.

Behind her, it wasn't much quieter. MPs cupped their hands to their mouths and hooted across the chamber. The wooden benches reverberated with hands slapped on their backs, and air gusted towards her as people leaned forwards in their places.

Beside her, John was quiet.

She waited for the noise to subside. It didn't.

"Order!" the Speaker cried, reddening.

The shouts were replaced by whispers. She took another breath and glanced at her notes. She didn't need them.

She pulled back her shoulders. Time to perform.

"I have a statement to make about recent events at Bronzefield Prison," she began.

The noise started up again.

"This House is aware of the unfortunate and tragic death of Hayley Price, one of Bronzefield's inmates."

More shouting. *What must we look like to the outside world?* she thought. This was nothing to get excited about. A woman was dead.

Hayley had been just nineteen years old, arrested for stealing from a pharmacy. She'd wanted the drugs to abort an unwanted pregnancy. On remand at Bronzefield, she'd somehow got hold of a coat hanger. The results – Jennifer had seen the photos – hadn't been pretty.

Poor girl. Only five years older than Samir. She wondered what Hayley's mother was going through.

She looked at the Speaker, who was calling for order. When the noise calmed, she kept her voice low.

"Thank you, Mr Speaker. I would like to ask my honourable friends to join me in showing respect for Hayley's memory and sympathy for her family at what must be a dreadful time for them.

"Hayley Price was a vulnerable young woman imprisoned when she should have been helped."

Muttering from behind her. She lifted her chin higher.

"At nineteen years of age, Hayley found herself pregnant." She paused to look around her colleagues. John was still, staring ahead. She sniffed and raised her voice, aware of the impact of her words. "She tried to end that pregnancy, but found herself on the wrong side of the law. Which is how she ended up at Bronzefield."

Just out of her line of vision, she sensed John turn towards her. She licked her lips.

They want me to apologise, she thought. *They want me to make excuses*.

That wasn't going to happen. She continued.

"Hayley tried again to end her pregnancy, but instead she died. In the most brutal, bleak and lonely circumstances we can imagine any young person dying in." She paused, allowing the words to sink in. "We must never allow that to happen again. As a civilised society, we have a duty to protect all of our citizens. Even those who break the law. And especially those who are most vulnerable."

She looked around her colleagues. *I'm not going anywhere*, she thought. "I will work to ensure that our prisons are not only places of security but places of safety too. Where offenders will receive the sentence they have been handed down, but no more."

She looked up and across the chamber. Her hands were still together but loosely now. No-one was shouting, or jeering, or even muttering. The chamber was quiet.

None of the MPs surrounding her had the slightest idea what it would be like to be Hayley Price. Raised by a mother who'd never held down a job, pregnant at nineteen, a criminal.

Jennifer knew more about it than most of them. Left alone with her mother at six years old, after her father had walked out. She still didn't know why. If she hadn't found Yusuf, who knows where she might have ended up?

She looked at the Speaker. "Mr Speaker, if you would permit me an indulgence on Hayley's behalf."

He nodded.

"I would like the House to join me in a minute's silence so we can remember Hayley and consider how we can prevent another tragic death like hers."

There was rustling as people looked around, then

bowed their heads or placed their hands in their laps. Jennifer stayed standing for the minute, listing to the faint tick of her wristwatch. At last the Speaker coughed.

"Thank you," she said, and sat down. She felt John's hand on her shoulder and turned to see him nod.

~

She arrived in the Members' Dining Room at a quarter past twelve.

As she passed between the tables, she sensed a hush descend over the MPs. A few people got up to congratulate her. She thanked them as graciously as she could, but felt awkward and undeserving. She'd rescued her career, but it hadn't helped Hayley.

John was late. After choosing some fish and salad from the buffet, she chose a quiet corner table and took the seat facing the room. Then she bent to her bag and grabbed her phone.

She soon exhausted her inbox and picked up a fork, looking around the room. Her gaze rested on a white-haired man sitting at a window table with three expensively suited companions. As his companions talked, his gaze was fixed on the room. His eyes flickered around, registering each of the other diners as they arrived or departed, taking them in with a curled lip. The white hair framed a copper-coloured face, the forehead a touch too smooth and shiny. Botox, she suspected. His bright blue eyes and the thin line of his lips were barely visible against his perma-tanned skin. Looking at him always made Jennifer think of cheap American soap operas.

The man was Leonard Trask, Leader of the Opposition. On TV, that smirk looked like a smile, and the tan became a healthy glow. But in person, the effect was different.

Jennifer stared at him despite herself, regretting it when his eye caught hers. He smiled. She held his gaze for a moment, then pretended to be answering a call.

She kept her head down until John arrived, scrolling through Twitter as she ate. She was trending.

John hurried in, exchanging greetings and pausing for brief conversations. He threw her a nod before helping himself to a salad and making his way to their table.

Jennifer looked at his plate and raised an eyebrow. John laughed. "Surprised? Got to do something about this, eh?" He rubbed his belly. A hard-won belly, acquired through years of socialising in the dining rooms and bars of this place.

Jennifer settled into her chair, waiting. John leaned back and surveyed her.

"Well done," he said.

She smiled, relieved. "Thank you."

"I think you saved the day."

She shrugged; it wouldn't do to crow.

"So," he continued. "What's happening at the prison?"

"I've spoken to Sandra Phipps. The governor," she said. "I'm going tomorrow."

He cocked his head. "You haven't already been?"

"It only happened yesterday morning."

"Or the night before."

"I know." She sighed. "But I only found out yesterday morning."

"Before or after the press?"

She closed her eyes for a moment. The previous day she had been woken at six am by a call from the office. Quickly followed by a call from the Daily Telegraph.

"That's hardly the issue."

"It makes us look bloody incompetent, you know. If you hadn't—"

"Yes, but I did."

He sighed. "You're right." He held up his hands in defeat. "I know, I know. You did well. Michael's pleased."

She wasn't sure how to respond; she and Michael had never exactly clicked. "Good."

"Indeed. Anyway, let's get these bloody salads down us and back to work."

She let herself relax. "Did I tell you it's Hassan's birthday?"

"Hmm?"

She smiled. "Yusuf's brought him and Samir down to London for a couple of days. A treat."

"Oh. Good, good." John knew her family; Yusuf had worked for him as a researcher in John's first term as an MP. Back then it was Yusuf who was the ambitious one, the future MP. But fatherhood had changed him, and now he was more than content running a homeless shelter in Birmingham city centre. Jennifer admired his skill with people, the way he made those at their most desperate feel better about themselves, and the relationships he'd built locally. And he admired her ability to talk her way out of corners, like she had this morning. She'd learned to stand up for herself as a child, realising no-one else was going to do it for her.

"They're on the London Eye, this afternoon." She frowned. "Or maybe getting a pizza, I can't remember which was first."

"Nice," John replied, glancing at his watch. He started to push himself up, but then something in the mirror behind her caught his eye. He sat down again.

She looked over his shoulder to see a uniformed security guard weaving between the tables, heading for them. John's eyes were trained on her face; he looked worried. What was going on?

John stood and turned as the man reached them. There was a whispered conversation between them. John's features clouded as he listened.

He turned to her.

"We'll have to continue this later," he said. "I'm needed. And you've got to go to Committee Room 14. Right now."

Around the dining room there was a flurry of movement: people pulling phones out of pockets, bending to retrieve them from bags and briefcases. Jennifer's own phone buzzed on the table.

"Why?" she asked.

Ministers were rising from their tables. Backbench MPs watched them, confused. Jennifer saw one of the ministers shake his head at a junior colleague. Their gazes shifted to John.

John shook his head. "Can't tell you. Not yet. Just go."

He marched out of the room, looking straight ahead.

OCTOBER 2019. LONDON

THE COMMITTEE ROOM WAS FILLING UP WITH LABOUR
MPs by the time she arrived, the crush of bodies making the
room feel damp with sweat.

She scanned the room for clues as to why they'd been
summoned here. Officials darted in and out, searching the
crowd and making notes but not stopping for long enough to
speak to anyone. Groups came together then broke apart,
new huddles forming in a kind of dance. The room was
filled with the hum of low conversation; rumours, questions,
speculation. *Facts?*

It was as full as a controversial meeting of the Parliamentary Labour Party, and almost as deafening. But no one
was sitting on the long wooden benches: instead, they all
shifted around the outer edges of the room, newcomers
holding their breath to squeeze past colleagues.

She pushed through, muttering the occasional hello.
People weren't interested in her now; she was old news. She
wanted to know who was here. It didn't take her long to
realise that there wasn't a single Cabinet member and not
many of her own rank. It was mainly backbenchers.

She had a moment of panic, then pushed it away. John had sent her here, and he knew – even if no one else did – that she hadn't been relegated to the backbenches. Besides, after her reception in the chamber this morning, surely no one would expect...

She leaned against the wood panelled wall. Her palms were dry and her feet ached in her stiff new shoes. A vicarious birthday present from Yusuf.

She felt a hand on her shoulder and looked up, tensing. It was someone from the Serjeant at Arms office, the team that administered the building.

He smiled. "Minister, would you like to take a seat? We could be here for a while."

She opened her mouth to ask a question. But he was gone, weaving his way through the crush and tapping the occasional junior ministerial shoulder.

She looked at the benches. They were all but empty, with only a few elderly and one pregnant MP sitting down. Each of them sat alone, staring ahead in silence or jabbing at their phones for news.

She fished her own phone out of her bag, scrolling through Twitter. She was still trending, although the attention was starting to dip. But there was nothing to explain what was happening here, why they'd all been summoned. No one had leaked it, yet.

A group of men drifted towards her, pushed by the swelling crowd. She pretended to stare at her phone's screen while she listened in to their conversation.

"Tony from The Times says there's a terror threat. Nothing confirmed yet."

"I've seen pictures of police vans at Waterloo."

Waterloo?

She looked towards the tall windows. People were

crowding towards them, maybe hearing the same rumours. She fought her way through the wall of suits, ignoring people's muttered complaints, until she emerged beside the window.

She pressed the palm of her hand against the window, the mullioned lead cold to the touch. Outside, the city looked much as it ever did. Tourist boats made their way up and down the Thames, windows glinting in the sunshine. On the opposite bank, runners and idle strollers wove around each other. And beyond that, in the direction of Waterloo station and her own flat, dark buildings rose up, the skyscrapers of the City looming behind them.

The crowd had tightened behind her; she couldn't have moved if she'd wanted to. People jabbed their elbows into each other and tripped over each other's feet in an effort to stay upright.

A rumble came from outside and she felt the weight of the crowd as people leaned to see out. She threw out an arm to steady herself, her breathing short. Another rumble: this time the crowd stilled, staring out and across the river.

Beyond the water, beyond the tourists and the London Eye, smoke gushed up and over the rooftops, spreading and billowing as the wind caught it. She stared as it thickened and rose. Behind her was silence, the Parliamentary Labour Party collectively holding its breath.

The cloud cleared the rooftops and the breeze pulled it in their direction. The buildings surrounding Waterloo station disappeared from view, followed by County Hall and the pods of the London Eye.

She felt her chest hollow out. The London Eye!

She fell back into the crowd, clutching her throat.

What had Yusuf told her this morning? The Eye and then a pizza. *Maybe you can join us later?*

She stared at the oversized Ferris wheel. Tiny figures moved inside the highest pod, the one at the very apex of the wheel. She lost sight of it as the cloud rose to envelop it, pitching it and the other pods in a grey-brown haze.

She stared at it for a few moments, blinking. She span round and clawed her way through the crowd. "Get out of my way!" She didn't care whose feet she trampled, felt no concern about bodies stumbling as she pushed them aside. She had to get out of here – get to her children.

She stumbled into the back of a bench, her knuckles grazing on the worn wood. She caught herself and managed to take a shaky breath, massaging her temples, willing the images out of her head. Images of Yusuf and the boys in that pod, staring into the dark cloud. *Stay calm*, she told herself. *You're no use to them like this*. Samir clutching Yusuf's hand despite his maturity and Hassan's little fingers pulsing in his dad's. So easy to lose their grip in the darkness and the panic...

She shook the images from her head, gasping. She fumbled her bag open and delved inside for her phone. Trembling, she brought up her favourites and jabbed at Yusuf's name. It took two attempts to hit the right key.

She clutched the phone to her ear, eyes darting around the room. Even the elderly MPs had left their seats and were standing at the back of the throng, trying to see what was going on. Just Mary Boulding, eight months pregnant and barely mobile, sat alone in the centre of the room.

The phone was silent. She pulled it from her ear and looked at the display. No service. She screwed up her face and tried again. Her breaths were shortening, becoming little more than gasps.

A woman passed her, floral perfume wafting in her wake. Jennifer gagged.

She bent over, willing the nausea to subside.

When she'd regained control of her breathing and felt she could move again, she looked on the floor for her phone. There it lay, next to her foot, the white light on its side blinking.

She grabbed it. Yusuf?

No. It was an email from 10 Downing Street, an automated circular with details of tomorrow's events. The wifi was still working, then.

She opened WhatsApp and barked out a quick note to Yusuf. *Are you OK? Call or message me. I'm at work.* She stared at the screen, waiting for a response. She considered for a moment then forwarded it to Samir. He never picked up her messages but it was worth a try.

She lowered herself onto a bench, throwing her head back and her gaze up to the ceiling. Overhead, the ornate carvings stared impassively down at her. This room – this building – had seen other days like this.

The crowd had shifted to one end of the room and was facing the raised platform at the front where committee chairs and witnesses or guest speakers normally sat. Once again she was faced with a wall of backs.

She approached it, puzzled. Then she heard a familiar voice.

"Good afternoon, everyone."

John.

She squeezed through the crush. *I'm a Home Office minister*, she thought. *I need to be up there*.

John coughed then took a long swig from a bottle someone passed up to him. His tie was askew and his shirt had damp patches under the arms.

He whistled out a breath and passed the water to an

advisor. There was a sheet of paper in his hand but he didn't look at it.

"Sorry to keep you in here, everyone."

Murmurs surrounded her.

He looked around his audience, his eyes alighting on Jennifer. He allowed his gaze to rest on her face for a few beats too long, then looked away.

He looked towards the window. The muttering stopped. "There's been an explosion," he said. "In Waterloo tube station."

Jennifer felt her legs go weak. She tried to pull her phone out of her pocket but couldn't move her arms in the crush.

"We don't know the details yet," John said, taking another swig of water. "And we couldn't tell you all of it if we did."

Gasps ran through the crowd. John raised a hand to ask for quiet.

"That's not all," he said, his voice turning grave. He looked at Jennifer again, his eyes searching her face. "There's been another one. Roughly the same time." His eyes were drilling into Jennifer now. She shifted her weight, hearing a tut as her heel spiked someone's shoe.

"Spaghetti Junction," John managed to say. Jennifer stared back at him, her pulse throbbing behind her eyes.

Spaghetti Junction.

Gravelly Hill Interchange.

In her Birmingham constituency.

John watched her as he spoke. It was as if they were the only people in the room. She gave him a single nod. *Go on. Tell me more.*

He didn't break eye contact. "Before the explosion at Waterloo there was one at Spaghetti Junction. Not as big as the one here in London," he nodded towards the window, "but it's chaos."

She closed her eyes. Around her people were talking in whispers, gasps and murmurs. She opened her eyes to see John looking away, deep in conversation with a man she didn't recognise. One of his political advisors was at his back, trying to get him out of the room.

John reached behind, batting the hand away. He turned back to the crowd.

"You all need to stay here until we can give you clearance to leave." He looked around at the gathered faces, the people who trusted him. "Everyone. The building's in lockdown. "

A HOUSE DIVIDED

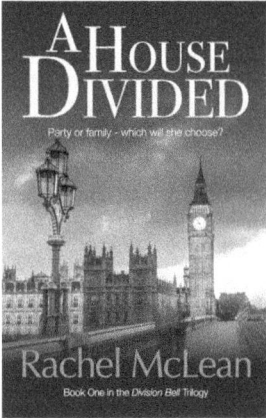

What if the government you served came for your family?

Jennifer Sinclair is many things: ambitious politician, loving wife and devoted mother.

But when the government she serves targets her Muslim husband and sons, where will her loyalties lie?

Can she hold her family together? And can she keep her children safe?

A House Divided is a gripping political thriller that's been described as 'virtual reality in book form'.

Buy Now on Amazon